LIES...BETRAYAL...SCANDA

Looks like the Ashton family is a little bigger than first thought...

It seems that Walker Ashton's past isn't what he thought it to be. Apparently he and his sister, Charlotte, had been lied to for years, and now he's feeling betrayed. After learning that the mother he thought long dead is in fact alive and well, the interim CEO of Ashton-Lattimer has left the boardroom to run off to a Native American reservation in Pine Ridge, South Dakota, to find the mother he was denied as a child. Wonder how that family reunion will play out!

And speaking of family reunions, or rather, reconciliations, what are the chances of Walker and his cousin Trace, who have always been at odds, ever coming to terms with each other? I mean, can the animosity between a father, his son and the father's favorite protégé ever be fully forgiven, or will the bitter betrayal of birthrights bring down the business?
Stay tuned....

Dear Reader,

July is a month known for its heat and fireworks, as well as the perfect time to take that vacation. Well, why not take a break and enjoy some hot sparks with a Silhouette Desire? We've got six extraordinary romances to share with you this month, starting with *Betrayed Birthright* by Sheri WhiteFeather. This seventh title in our outstanding DYNASTIES: THE ASHTONS series is sure to reveal some unbelievable facts about this scandalous family.

USA TODAY bestselling author Maureen Child wraps up her fabulous THREE-WAY WAGER series with *The Last Reilly Standing.* Or is he getting down on bended knee? And while some series are coming to a close, new ones are just beginning, such as our latest installment of the TEXAS CATTLEMAN'S CLUB: THE SECRET DIARY. Cindy Gerard kicks off this six-book continuity with *Black-Tie Seduction.* Also starting this month is Bronwyn Jameson's PRINCES OF THE OUTBACK. These Australian hunks really need to be tamed, beginning with *The Rugged Loner.*

A desert beauty in love with a tempting beast. That's the theme of Nalini Singh's newest release, *Craving Beauty*—a story not to be missed. And the need to break a long-standing family curse leads to an attraction that's just *Like Lightning,* an outstanding romance by Charlene Sands.

Here's hoping you enjoy all the fireworks Silhouette Desire has to offer you…this month and all year long!

Best,

Melissa Jeglinski

Melissa Jeglinski
Senior Editor
Silhouette Desire

Please address questions and book requests to:
Silhouette Reader Service
U.S.: 3010 Walden Ave., P.O. Box 1325, Buffalo, NY 14269
Canadian: P.O. Box 609, Fort Erie, Ont. L2A 5X3

BETRAYED BIRTHRIGHT

Sheri WhiteFeather

Silhouette® Desire

Published by Silhouette Books

America's Publisher of Contemporary Romance

Special thanks and acknowledgment are given to
Sheri WhiteFeather for her contribution to
the DYNASTIES: THE ASHTONS series.

SILHOUETTE BOOKS

ISBN 0-373-76663-7

BETRAYED BIRTHRIGHT

This edition published by arrangement with Harlequin Books S.A.

® and TM are trademarks of Harlequin Books S.A., used under license.
Trademarks indicated with ® are registered in the United States Patent
and Trademark Office, the Canadian Trade Marks Office and in other
countries.

Visit Silhouette Books at www.eHarlequin.com

Printed in U.S.A.

SHERI WHITEFEATHER

lives in Southern California and enjoys ethnic dining, attending powwows and visiting art galleries and vintage clothing stores near the beach. Since her one true passion is writing, she is thrilled to be a part of the Silhouette Desire line. When she isn't writing, she often reads until the wee hours of the morning.

Sheri's husband, a member of the Muscogee Creek Nation, inspires many of her stories. They have a son, a daughter and a trio of cats—domestic and wild. She loves to hear from her readers. You may write to her at: P.O. Box 17146, Anaheim, California 92817. Visit her Web site at www.SheriWhiteFeather.com.

THE ASHTONS

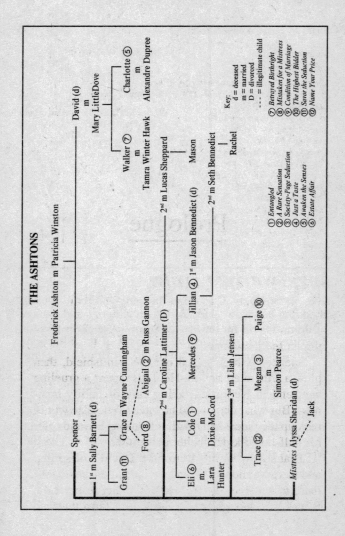

Frederick Ashton m Patricia Winston

Spencer

David (d) m Mary LittleDove

1st m Sally Barnett (d)

Grant ⑪

Grace m Wayne Cunningham

Abigail ② m Russ Gannon

Ford ⑧

Cole ①
m
Dixie McCord

2nd m Caroline Lattimer (D)

Mercedes ⑨

Eli ⑥
m.
Lara Hunter

Jillian ④ 1st m Jason Bennedict (d)

2nd m Seth Bennedict

Mason

Rachel

3rd m Lilah Jensen

Megan ③
m
Simon Pearce

Paige ⑩

Trace ⑫

Mistress Alyssa Sheridan (d)

Jack

Walker ⑦
m
Tamra Winter Hawk

2nd m Lucas Sheppard

Charlotte ⑤
m
Alexandre Dupree

Key:
d = deceased
m = married
D = divorced
--- = Illegitimate child

① Entangled
② A Rare Sensation
③ Society-Page Seduction
④ Just a Taste
⑤ Awaken the Senses
⑥ Estate Affair
⑦ Betrayed Birthright
⑧ Mistaken for a Mistress
⑨ Condition of Marriage
⑩ The Highest Bidder
⑪ Savor the Seduction
⑫ Name Your Price

Prologue

1983

Damn David for dying. And damn him for marrying an Indian woman.

Spencer Ashton gazed out the windshield, then blew a frustrated breath. He'd just spent a grueling weekend in Nebraska, taking care of family business. But what choice did he have? Who else would pick up the pieces of David's crumbled life and offer his half-breed kids a better existence?

That squaw wasn't fit to raise David's offspring, and there was no way Spencer would allow her to take them to her freeloading, war-whooping reservation. It was bad enough they'd lived on a farm that had never prospered, a farm Spencer had helped David buy long before he'd married Mary Little Dove.

But in the end, David had been too proud to admit that he and his family were starving.

Spencer flipped the sun visor, squinting into the afternoon light. He was on his way home from the airport, heading to Napa Valley, California, where he owned a thriving winery and a twenty-two-thousand-square-foot mansion. The boy and girl he'd acquired—his dead brother's children—sat next to him in the front seat of his luxury sedan.

He glanced over and saw that three-year-old Charlotte was still behaving like a lost bird. She even chirped every so often, grating on his nerves. He'd tried to put her in the backseat, but she wouldn't leave her big brother's side. Spencer had no use for wounded creatures, but what could he do? She was David's daughter.

The eight-year-old boy, on the other hand, had already garnered Spencer's respect. Walker held his head high. The kid had moxie. Balls. He deserved to be an Ashton.

Too bad he was part Indian.

But Spencer would find a way to get past that. Not that he favored children, Lord knew he had enough of his own. He even had another baby on the way, but Walker was different. He would probably prove to be better than any of Spencer's kids.

Charlotte made another nervous sound, and Spencer gripped the steering wheel.

"She's scared," Walker said.

"Yes, of course. Your parents are gone." Or so they had been told. Their mother was still alive, but that was Spencer's secret. Everyone, except his lawyer, had been fed the same story: Mary Little Dove had died from injuries she'd sustained in an automobile accident, just like David.

Spencer and his attorney had strong-armed her into giving up her kids, but it had been the right thing to do.

Walker was proof. The boy looked dapper in the clothes Spencer had purchased for him. And he hadn't balked about getting his hair cut, either. Spencer wasn't about to take the kids home looking like a couple of ragamuffins.

He turned to study the boy's posture. Although he protected his sister, keeping her close, he still had an air of independence. His mother had called him a warrior. A Sioux at heart. But Spencer sensed otherwise. This kid should have been white.

"I was poor when I was young, too," Spencer said. "But I wanted something better."

Walker glanced up. "My dad talked about you."

"Did he?"

"Yes, sir."

"I would have saved his farm. I didn't know it was in foreclosure, that he was losing it." Spencer knew what people said about him: that he was a bastard, a self-righteous prick. But what the hell did they know? He'd always done right by David, even if his kid brother had been a sentimental fool. "I tried to help your dad succeed."

"And now you're helping me and Charlotte," Walker said.

"That's right, I am. Without me, you and your sister wouldn't have a home."

"I've been praying for Mom and Dad."

Normal prayers, Spencer hoped. None of that heathen crap.

Walker glanced out the window. He had a chiseled profile—handsome, in spite of his brown skin. He seemed to be surveying the land, the wealth of the wine country. Spencer suspected he appreciated what he saw. This kid would be grateful for his uncle's generosity.

"Is my dad going to be buried here?" Walker asked.

"Yes, he is."

"And my mom?"

"No, son. She'll be laid to rest on that Indian reservation. The place where she came from. But it's too far away for you to attend the funeral."

"I've never been there."

And you never will, Spencer thought. He noticed the eight-year-old's voice had turned raw, but he wouldn't dare cry. He was too strong to bawl, to act like a baby. Nope, Walker Ashton wasn't a sniffling coward.

It was hard to believe that mealy-mouthed Sioux had given birth to him. She'd fallen apart at the seams, no backbone whatsoever. But just to ensure she kept up her end of the bargain, Spencer had arranged a thirty-thousand-dollar payment.

A pittance in his bankbook, a fortune in hers.

As for Walker and Charlotte, he supposed they were worth a few bucks. The boy was, anyway. The timid little girl merely came with the deal.

But it was the best deal either of them would ever get. As far as Spencer was concerned, he'd done himself proud.

One

Walker wished his sister had never found out that their mother was still alive. And worse yet, he wished Charlotte hadn't convinced him to look for her.

He sat on the edge of his motel-room bed and blew a weary breath. He was staying in Gordon, Nebraska, but he'd been scouting the South Dakota reservation, traveling from district to district, cursing Pine Ridge, a place that encompassed two million acres and some of the poorest counties in the nation.

He would just as soon forget about that Native American hellhole, let alone claim to part of the Oglala Lakota Sioux Nation. While his sister had romantic notions about Indians, Walker was a realist. A liquored-up Native loitering in one of the paltry little towns had called him a stupid *iyeska* when he'd nearly stumbled over the man's prone form.

Iyeska.

It was an insult he couldn't even translate.

Hot and tired, he unbuttoned his shirt and untucked it from his jeans, preparing to take a shower, to wash the grime from his body. He wasn't used to the sweltering heat, to the depressing vastness of the land.

When a knock sounded, Walker came to his feet, anxiety knotting his stomach. He'd left word with postal workers, BIA employees, anyone who seemed educated enough to listen. He'd even spoken with tribal cops, but no one had been particularly helpful. If anything, they'd treated him with indifference. The way he'd treated them, he supposed.

He answered the door and stared at the woman on the other side. He hadn't expected his visitor to be young and beautiful. She stood about five-seven, with shoulder-length black hair and exotic brown eyes.

She wore a simple blouse and a pair of nondescript shorts, but her legs—

When she raised her eyebrows at him, he quit checking her out and remembered that his shirt was unbuttoned, exposing his chest and the sweat dampening his skin.

Uncomfortable, he frowned at her, wondering if she thought he was an *iyeska,* too. Clearly, she was Indian, probably from the reservation.

"Are you Walker Ashton?" she asked.

"Yes." He wanted to wipe his hands on his jeans. He didn't like feeling disorganized and dirty. As the interim CEO of Ashton-Lattimer, an investment banking firm in San Francisco, he relied on cell phones, e-mails, fax transmittals and designer suits.

She tilted her head. "I'm Tamra Winter Hawk. I live with Mary Little Dove Ashton."

His anxiety worsened. Deep down he'd hoped that he wouldn't find his mom. That he could tell Charlotte that he'd done his best but a family reunion wasn't meant to be.

He shifted his stance. "How long have you lived with her?"

"Mary took me in when I was a child."

"I see." His mom had raised someone else's kid while his baby sister had longed for maternal affection? That pissed him off, even if the details weren't clear. "I'd like to speak with her."

"She's at work. And she doesn't know that you're looking for her. She has no idea you're here."

"But you do." Apparently someone had told Tamra about the city-slick stranger who'd been poking around, driving from one poverty-laden county to the next, claiming to be Mary's long-lost son. "So what's the problem? Why are you keeping her from me?"

Tamra didn't respond. With her striking features and regal posture, she reminded Walker of a museum bronze, an untouchable object encased in glass.

"I'd like to see your ID," she finally said.

He squinted into the sun, the hot, fiery ball blazing behind her. "What for?"

"To make sure you're who you say you are."

Who the hell else would he be? A government

agent on the verge of breaking a treaty? Why would he sacrifice his time—his valuable time—to traipse across this godforsaken land if he wasn't Mary's son?

He glared at her. If the police hadn't asked for his ID, then why should she? "I don't need to prove anything to you."

"Then maybe I should leave." Much too elusive, she turned away, her hair spinning in a dark circle.

Walker wanted to let her go, but he knew he couldn't. Charlotte would never forgive him.

Frustrated, he removed his wallet and followed her into the parking lot. "Hold on."

Tamra stopped to face him. For a moment he was struck by how easily she'd managed to stir his blood, to fuel his temper.

Walker didn't let women get under his skin.

Once again she reminded him of a bronze statue. Beautiful, breathtaking, far too aloof. Too bad he'd been taught to behave in museums, he thought. To keep his hands off the glass.

"Will you take it out?" she asked.

Take what out? he wondered, as his brain went numb.

She waited, and he blinked away his confusion. She then asked him to remove his ID from his wallet.

Complying with her request, he handed her his driver's license. She scanned his identification, studying the photo. He knew it was a lousy picture. But those Department of Motor Vehicles cameras weren't meant to be flattering.

"Satisfied?" he asked, his unbuttoned shirt sticking to his skin.

She returned his license. "I'll talk to Mary when she gets home from work."

"Then what?"

"I'll call you and let you know when you can see her."

Right, he thought. Because Mary was queen of the reservation. Or the rez. Or whatever the term for that ghetto plain was.

Aware of his animosity, Tamra sighed. "Your mother has been hurt. I'm only trying to protect her."

No kidding? Well, he'd been hurt, too. He had no idea why Spencer had lied to him years ago, telling him that his mom was dead. And now Spencer was dead, gunned down by an unknown assailant.

Walker's emotions were a flat-out mess.

He motioned to his room, where he'd left the door open. "I'll be here. Do you need the number?"

"No, thanks. I already have it." She paused, her voice turning soft. "Please don't be angry, Walker. At least, not at Mary. She never quit missing you and Charlotte."

His chest constricted, making it tough to breathe.

When he and Charlotte first moved in with Spencer, he used to whisper in the dark, telling her that Mommy and Daddy were angels, watching them from above. But eventually he'd settled into his new life, and he'd quit consoling his sister about the parents they'd lost.

Spencer had become Walker's mentor, the only

person he'd strived to impress. He'd chosen the older man over everyone, including Charlotte, leaving her to fend for herself.

"I'm not angry," he said. But he was, of course. Somewhere in the pit of his stomach, he was mad as hell.

At himself, at Spencer, at Mary.

And at her, too. Tamra Winter Hawk.

The girl his mother had raised.

While the aroma of beef stew wafted through the house, Tamra helped Mary tidy the living room, dusting, vacuuming and fluffing pillows.

Mary turned off the vacuum and looked around. "This place is dingy, isn't it? No matter what we do, it's still an old mobile home."

"It's the same age as me. And I'm not old." Besides, they had cozy furniture, indoor plumbing, heat in the winter and plenty of food in the icebox. To Tamra that was enough.

But she knew how nervous Mary was. She'd been clucking around like a chicken in the rain, preparing for her son but drowning in the fear of seeing him.

"Tell me about him, Tamra. Tell me about Walker."

What could she say that would put the other woman at ease? "He'll be here in about an hour, Mary."

"I know, but I want to know what you thought of him. You never gave me your opinion."

That was true. She hadn't told Mary that he'd triggered her emotions. Or that his intensity reminded her of the past, of the years she'd spent in San Francisco, of the man who'd destroyed her heart.

She glanced at Mary, saw that she waited for a response. "He's stunning." Tall and lean, she thought, with just the right blend of power, of male muscle. "He was dressed casually." And she'd noticed his chest, his stomach, the indentation of his navel. "But he doesn't seem like a casual guy."

Mary frowned. "You could tell he was rich?"

"Yes."

"Fancy watch? Designer labels on his clothes?"

Tamra nodded, troubled by the insecurity in the other woman's eyes. "But you know what?" she said, hoping to soften the blow. "He looks like his dad." She'd seen photographs of David Ashton. She knew all about the farmer Mary had married. "And he resembles you, too."

Walker's mother relaxed a little. "He looked like both of us when he was young." She paused, took an audible breath. "Do you think he'll like stew?"

"Sure." And if he didn't, she doubted he would say otherwise. He would probably go through the motion of being polite. Of course, he hadn't been particularly polite with Tamra. But she'd been harsh with him. She didn't trust his motives, and she suspected he was going to complicate their lives.

Turn their Lakota world on its ear.

Most whitemanized Indians were brash and unyielding. Tamra knew because she'd been one herself. And in some ways she was still struggling with her identity.

"I wonder why he didn't mention Charlotte," Mary said. "Are you sure he didn't say anything about his sister?"

"I'm sure. But you can ask him about her."

"Yes, of course." Nervous once again, Mary smoothed her blouse. She'd chosen a floral-printed top and blue pants, an outfit she'd purchased last summer. She didn't fuss over her clothes and she rarely wore makeup. But this evening she'd put on lipstick. And she'd curled her rain-straight hair.

But even so, she looked older than her fifty-seven years. Her beauty had faded. Tamra had watched it dissipate. Mary had lived a hard life, and the lines in her face bore the brunt of her labor.

The pain of losing her children.

And now Walker was back. A stranger. A man with a distant heart. He hadn't asked about his mom. Nothing that gave Tamra an indication that he cared.

"I'll make the salad," she said, needing to keep busy. The anticipation of entertaining Walker was making her anxious, too.

"I'll bet he's used to steak and lobster." Mary put the vacuum cleaner into the hall closet, then frowned at their cluttered kitchen, at the simplicity of their existence. "Do you think Spencer knows he's here?"

"I have no idea." Tamra knew that Spencer Ashton had taken Walker and Charlotte away from their mother. He was responsible for the constant ache in Mary's chest, for the tears she'd cried.

Tamra washed her hands, running them under the

cold water. She couldn't help being fiercely protective of the woman who'd raised her.

"Is it too hot in here?" Mary asked, stirring the stew. "Should we open another window?"

"It's starting to cool off. It'll be okay."

"Will it?"

"Yes." She hated the shame that had begun to creep into their minds. Tamra and Mary had strived to accept their lifestyle, to be proud of it.

Mary set the table, but when Walker arrived, she was in the bathroom, reapplying her lipstick.

Tamra answered the knock on the screen door, and for a moment she and Walker gazed at each other through the barrier.

He didn't smile. He looked impeccably groomed in a tan shirt and matching trousers. He was cleanly shaven and his short dark hair was combed away from his face, exposing his half-blood features.

Tamra's pulse zigzagged, like invisible footprints racing up her arm.

The last man who'd had that kind of effect on her had given her a child. A baby she'd buried in San Francisco, the city where Walker lived.

"Come in," she said, opening the screen door. It wasn't a fluke that Tamra was connected to San Francisco. That she'd spent her college years there. She'd chosen that region because of Walker and his sister.

"Thanks." He entered the house, then handed her a bouquet of roses. "I was going to bring a bottle of wine, but since they don't sell alcohol on the reservation, I figured you weren't allowed to indulge in it, either." He paused, shrugged a little. "But I've seen plenty of people drinking. I guess everyone doesn't follow the rules."

She merely nodded. The white-owned liquor stores in the border towns catered to Lakota drunks. His mother was far too familiar with that scenario to think of alcohol as a luxury, even an exceptional bottle of wine. Mary's brother had died from alcoholism. "Your mom will appreciate the flowers."

"Where is she?"

"Freshening up. She'll only be a minute."

Or a second, she thought, as Mary appeared in the hallway.

Walker turned around, and Tamra watched mother and son face each other for the first time in twenty-two years.

Tears filled Mary's eyes, but she didn't step forward to hug her boy. He didn't embrace her, either.

Awkward silence stretched between them.

Walker didn't know what to say. Mary didn't look familiar. But he didn't have any old pictures, nothing to refresh his memory.

Was he a coldhearted bastard? Or was it normal that he didn't feel anything? That Mary Little Dove didn't seem like his mother?

When she blinked, the tears that were gathered on her lashes fluttered like raindrops. Should he offer her his handkerchief? Or would that trigger even more tears? Walker didn't want to make her cry.

He moved forward, just a little, stepping closer to her. Why had his memories faded? Why couldn't he see her in his mind? He remembered the farm, but he couldn't recall his mom.

Because it had been easier to forget, he thought. Easier to let her go, to get on with his life.

"My son," Mary said, breaking the silence. "My boy. I never thought I'd see you again. But here you are. So tall. So handsome."

A muscle clenched in his jaw. "We thought you were dead."

"I know." The tears glistening on her lashes fell, dotting her cheeks. "I'm aware of what Spencer told you."

She knew? She'd been part of the lie? Walker wanted to turn away, to shut her out of his life once again, but his feet wouldn't move. He simply stood there, the weight of her words dragging him down.

"Is Charlotte all right?" she asked. "Does she know you came to see me?"

"My sister is fine, and this was her idea."

Mary pressed her hand against her heart. "My baby girl. She was only three years old. How could she possibly remember me?"

Walker didn't respond. But how could he? He didn't remember her, either. And, God help him, he didn't want to. He had no desire to become her son, to be part of Pine Ridge, to embrace his Lakota roots.

Spencer had taught him that being Indian didn't matter. And from what Walker had seen so far, he had to agree.

He glanced at Tamra and saw that she watched him. Could she sense his thoughts? She clutched the roses he'd brought, and the bouquet made her look like a reservation bride, with a summer cotton dress flowing around her ankles.

"These are from Walker." She handed the roses to Mary.

His mother accepted the gift and smiled.

Walker took a deep breath. She looked pretty when she smiled. Softer, like the woman his father had probably fallen in love with. David Ashton had been a sentimental man, that much he knew. That much Spencer had told him.

"Thank you," Mary said to Walker.

He gave her a quick nod. "You're welcome."

"I'll make you a shield." She searched his gaze. "Your dad always wanted you to have one."

His white father wanted him to have a Lakota object? Walker didn't understand, but he tried to pretend that it made sense. He had no idea what he was supposed to do with a shield.

Declare war on another tribe? Hang it on his living room wall? Somehow he didn't see it complementing his contemporary decor. An interior designer had spent months laboring over his hillside condo.

Tamra spoke up. "The meal is ready. We should probably eat now."

"Yeah, sure." Anything to divert his mother's attention, he thought. To make her forget about the shield.

"I'll put these in water." Mary took the flowers

into the kitchen, where a simple table presented casual china, paper napkins and stainless steel flatware.

Walker waited for the women, intending to push in their chairs. But his mom tapped his shoulder and told him to sit, anxious to serve him. When she filled his glass with milk, he wondered if she'd forgotten that he was no longer eight years old.

Finally Mary and Tamra joined him, and they ate a hearty stew, an iceberg lettuce salad and rolls smothered in butter. It was the kind of meal a farmer's wife would prepare, he thought. Middle America. Only this was a South Dakota reservation.

He looked across the table at his mom. At Mary. His mind kept bouncing back and forth. He didn't know what to call her. How to refer to the woman who'd given him life.

"Did Spencer treat you well?" she asked.

He blinked, tried not to frown. "Yes. I was close to my uncle." And probably the only Ashton who could make that claim. No one had forged a bond with Spencer, not the way Walker did. But even so, it had been a hard-earned alliance. Spencer had been a complicated man.

"You're not close to him anymore?"

"Spencer is dead. He was murdered a few months ago. Shot to death in his office. Charlotte found his body."

"Oh, my. Oh." His mom fidgeted with her food. "I'm sorry. I'm so sorry."

When she stopped talking, the walls closed in. The kitchen was already cramped, the table too small for three people. Tamra sat next to him, too close for comfort.

He was still mourning his uncle, still missing him. Yet Spencer's betrayal kept him awake at night.

"Will you tell me about Charlotte?" Mary said.

He nodded, knowing how much this mattered to his sister. "She's engaged to Alexandre Dupree, a winemaker from France. He isn't the kind of man I'd envisioned for her, but they're crazy about each other." Madly in love, he supposed. "My sister was always shy, sort of dreamy. And Alexandre is—" he paused, trying to find a word to describe Charlotte's fiancé "—worldly."

"Like a prince." Mary sighed, already slipping into her daughter's fairy tale.

"I guess, yeah. Women probably think so." Walker knew that Alexandre had given his sister everything she needed, including the strength to investigate their family, to discover that Mary was still alive. "They're in Paris. Charlotte needed to get away after Spencer's funeral. But she made me promise that I'd search for you."

"I'm glad she did." Mary's eyes were watery again. "Do you have a picture of her?"

He shook his head. "I didn't think to bring one. But I'm sure she's going to rush back to meet you. Her and Alexandre."

"I can't wait to see her. And her fiancé, of course." Mary scooted closer to the table. "Is there someone special in your life, son?"

"Me?" Without thinking, he glanced at Tamra.

She turned toward him, and he shifted in his seat, wondering if she had a significant other, if she was sleeping with some big Indian buck.

Then he recalled the blonde in a San Francisco bar who'd tried to pin that phrase on him. A racial slur that had made him feel dirty.

"I'm not involved with anyone," he said. "I'm too busy with my career. Investment banking." More than ready to change the subject, he questioned his mom. "So, what kind of work do you do?"

She smoothed her gray-streaked hair. "I'm a nurse's aid at the PHS."

"PHS?"

"Public Health Service Hospital." She sat up a little straighter, proud of her job. "It's easier for me than some of the other aids. I lived in the white world, so I have a better understanding of the white doctors and nurses who work there."

Tamra interjected. "Most of the doctors are young. Physicians who received government loans for medical school. So they're paying back those loans by performing public health services on the reservation for a few years."

And probably hating every minute of it, he thought.

Tamra continued, "Our society equates wisdom with age, so it's difficult for our elders to accept young doctors. And there's often a language barrier. Far too many cultural differences." She glanced at his mom. "Mary is a valuable asset. The patients trust her. And so do the nurses and doctors."

Unsure of how to respond, he ate another a bite of stew. Mary sounded like a caring woman, yet she'd allowed her children to believe she was dead. He wanted to grill her about the past, to bombard her with accusations, but having Tamra nearby complicated the situation even more.

She'd taken his place. She'd been raised by the lady who'd let him go. And worse yet, he was attracted to Tamra.

A disaster in the making.

When he reached for his drink, he brushed her arm, a touch that made him much too aware.

"Sorry," he said. "I'm left-handed."

"It's okay." She tried to move away from him, to give him more room, but her effort proved useless. There was nowhere to go. They were stuck.

Yet his mother was smiling. "Walker used to do that when he was little, too."

"You mean this?" He lifted his milk, bumping Tamra's elbow, nearly knocking the roll out of her hand.

Everyone laughed. A silly incident. But it felt good. He hadn't laughed in a long time.

A few moments later, silence engulfed him. No one could think of anything to say, so they resumed their meal, making noise with spoons and forks and butter knives.

He glanced at a clock on the wall and imagined it ticking. Like a bomb, he thought. Like the day Spencer had taken legal custody of him and his sister, the day he'd been told that *both* of his parents had died.

Charlotte had been too young to understand, to com-

prehend the cold, harsh reality of never seeing Mommy
and Daddy again. But she'd cried just the same.

Walker stopped eating. His childhood memories
were scattered, lost in the darkness of his mind. But
not about that day. He remembered it vividly.

"Why did you do it?" he asked Mary, unable to
hold back his emotions, to keep faking this reunion.
"Why did you give us away?"

Two

"I'm sorry, Walker." Mary's voice quavered. "I should have explained everything right away. But I thought…I hoped…we could get to know each other first."

He pushed away his plate. "Why?"

"So you wouldn't judge me so harshly. So you wouldn't think I was trying to turn you against Spencer."

"I already told you. My uncle is dead."

"This is his fault," Tamra said. "He forced your mother to give up her children."

"Oh, yeah? With what? A gun?" Unable to sit at the cramped table any longer, he rose from his chair and glared at the young woman Mary had raised.

"Did he force her to take you in, too? To be your mom instead of ours?"

Tamra came to her feet. Suddenly she looked like a female warrior, her mouth set in a determined line, her dark eyes blazing with anger. "That isn't fair."

"You want to talk fair? There's no excuse for what my mom did. None whatsoever." He rounded on Mary. "I prayed for you. I called you an angel." Much too edgy, he blew out a hard breath. "When Spencer rescued us, I was so damn grateful. And so damn scared. Do you have any idea what being an orphan feels like?"

She didn't answer. She just swallowed the lump that seemed to be forming in her throat.

"I know what it feels like," Tamra said.

He spun around, gave her a cold look. "And that's supposed to make me feel better?"

"No. It's just that I understand."

"Yeah, right. You. The perfect Indian."

"Perfect?" She started clearing the table, moving at a frustrated pace. "You have no idea what I've been through. I wasn't raised in a mansion, Walker. My father ran off before I was born, and my mother was all alone, trying to survive on welfare. To find us suitable places to live."

"It's not the same thing." He gestured to Mary, who crossed her arms, hugging herself. "She let me think she was dead. At least your parents were honest."

"Don't point at her." Tamra clanked the dishes. "Don't do that. It's not proper."

"Says who? People on the rez?" As if he gave a

damn about Lakota etiquette. "Maybe someone should have told her that lying to her kids wasn't proper."

"Mary was on the verge of a breakdown when she lost your dad. And Spencer preyed on her emotions. He—"

Walker cut her off. He turned to his mom, needing to hear it from her. "Is that true?"

She nodded, and he realized how frail she looked, sitting alone at the table, listening to him and Tamra argue.

He resumed his seat, his heart pounding horribly in his chest. He wanted to call her a liar, but he knew his uncle had never tolerated gentle-natured women, especially when their wounds were still raw.

Yet he'd loved Spencer. He'd patterned his life after his father's power-hungry brother.

"Tell me," he said. "Tell me what he did."

"He came to see me in the hospital, right after your dad died. I was injured in the accident, nothing life threatening, but I still needed medical care."

"How did he force you to give us up?"

"He threatened me. He said he would get Social Services involved. That he would prove that I was an unfit mother."

"But you weren't." Walker studied the shadows under her eyes, the lines imbedded in her skin. "Were you?"

"Oh, God, no." She reached across the table and brushed his hand. A featherlight touch. The touch of a mother who'd lost her son. "I never abused my babies."

"I have no idea how you treated us." Which made Spencer's threats seem even more plausible, he thought. More frightening. "I can't remember you and Dad. I just can't."

"It's okay." Mary's voice went soft, sad. "It's been a long time."

"Yes, it has." Uncomfortable, he turned in his seat and noticed Tamra stood nearby. She'd fixed a pot of tea, some sort of herbal brew. When she offered him a cup, he looked up at her, and their gazes slammed straight into each other.

Heat. Emotion. The gates of Lakota hell.

He shouldn't be staring at her. Not like this.

Only, he couldn't seem to break eye contact.

And neither could she.

God help him, he thought. Suddenly he feared they were destined to be lovers, like misunderstood characters in a movie who yelled and screamed, then kissed like demons. He wasn't a fortune-teller. He couldn't predict the future. Yet he could feel the passion. The danger that awaited him.

He'd never been involved in a turbulent relationship. His affairs had never bordered on pain, on the kind of emotion that ripped a man apart.

But everything about Pine Ridge tore him in two.

Finally Tamra shifted her gaze, pouring Mary's tea. Afterward she sat next to Walker again, and he could smell the lotion on her skin, a disturbing blend of summer botanicals. A fragrance that made him want her even more.

Soft, airy, far too real.

Mary looked at both of them. "Neither of you deserve this."

"We can handle it." He turned to Tamra, then considered bumping her arm. But he knew no one would laugh this time. His left-handed antics wouldn't ease the tension. Nor would it change what was happening between him and Tamra.

"Yes," she agreed. "We can handle it."

Under the table, her leg was only inches from his, and the near contact made him warm. He didn't understand why she affected him so deeply, why she made him yearn for a forbidden liaison.

Was he trying to punish her? Or was he hell-bent on torturing himself?

"Finish your story," he said to Mary, trying to redirect his focus, to clear his head. "Tell me the rest."

"I was afraid of Spencer. Of his money, his power." She sipped her tea, clutching the cup with both hands. "When I was growing up, Lakota children were being put into foster care. Into white people's homes because their own families were too poor."

"And you thought Spencer could do that to us? That he could convince Social Services to take me and Charlotte?"

"Yes. I'd been away from the reservation for a long time. Married to your dad, being a farmer's wife. But in the end I was just a poor Indian all over again. Except, this time I was mourning my husband and drugged with painkillers from the hospital. I couldn't think clearly."

"But this was the eighties. Wasn't there something your tribe could have done to help you? To stop Spencer from taking us?"

"The Indian Child Welfare Act could have made a difference. But I didn't know about it then. It went into effect after I left the reservation." Her breath hitched, catching in her throat. "My life with your father was over. He was gone and the farm was in foreclosure. There was nowhere to go. Nowhere but here." She glanced at the window, where a small breeze stirred the curtains. "But at the time, all I had to come back to was a rundown shack and an alcoholic brother." She shifted her gaze. "Spencer threatened to use that against me. To drum up phony evidence that I was a drinker, too. That I hurt you and Charlotte. He knew people who would testify, who would lie for him."

Once again, Walker battled his confusion. He wished Mary had fought for her rights. That she'd done whatever she could to keep him and Charlotte. Yet he was glad Spencer had been his uncle.

"I didn't want my children growing up in foster care and thinking that I'd abused them," his mother said. "To me, that was worse than being dead."

Was it? Walker didn't know. He didn't have kids. He didn't have anything in his life but his work, the career Spencer had groomed him for.

"There's more," Mary told him. "Something else your uncle did. It seemed horrible at first. Only it didn't turn out to be a bad thing."

"Really? What was it?"

"Money." She nearly whispered, then raised her

voice a little louder. "His attorney sent me a thirty-thousand-dollar cashier's check after I got back to Pine Ridge. I didn't want to cash it at first."

"But eventually you did?"

"Yes." She reached for his hand. "I did."

Walker wanted to pull away from her. But he allowed her to touch him, feigning indifference, pretending that he could deal with the money.

With the sale of two small children….

The following day Tamra arrived at Walker's motel, per his request. He met her outside, looking like the city boy he was, with his well-tailored clothes and men's-fashion-magazine haircut. He wore the thick dark strands combed straight back and tamed with some sort of styling gel. Short but not conservative, at least not in a boring way.

Walker Ashton's hair had sex appeal.

"Hey," he said.

"Hey, yourself." She noticed that he seemed troubled. She hoped they wouldn't end up in another argument. "What's going on?"

"Nothing. I just want to talk." He reached into his pocket and removed some coins. "How about a soda?"

"Sure." She walked to the vending machine with him and chose an orange drink. He picked grape. From there, they headed back to his room.

She felt a bit odd going into the place where he'd been sleeping. She knew she shouldn't, but being with him in an intimate setting caused her heart to pound unmercifully in her breast.

She looked around his room and noticed the western motif. He'd chosen comfortable accommodations on Highway 20, but he was probably used to five-star hotels. This, she imagined, was foreign to him.

The window air conditioner was on full blast, with color streamers attached, blowing like international flags.

She sat at a pine table, and he leaned against the dresser, a big, sturdy unit that doubled as an entertainment center. She suspected that he'd climbed under the covers last night and watched cable TV.

What else would he do in a cozy Nebraska town?

"How old were you when my mom took you in?" he asked.

"I was five, but my mother was alive then. We both moved in with Mary. My mom and your mom were friends, and we didn't have anywhere else to go. It was winter. We would have frozen to death on our own." She flipped open the top of her soda, memories swirling in her mind. "My mom died two years later. So I was seven when Mary became my guardian."

"How old are you now?"

"Twenty-six."

A frown slashed between his eyebrows. "You're only a year older than my sister."

She nodded. Did that bother him? Did it make him feel even more betrayed? She wanted to ask him if he'd called his sister, if he'd spoken to her in France, but she decided to wait until he finished interviewing her. She could see the unanswered questions in his eyes.

"Is that common on the rez?" he asked. "To just raise someone else's kid?"

"Yes." She tried to relax, but he was making her self-conscious. The way he watched her. His hard-edged posture. "The Lakota have an adoption ceremony called Hunka, the making of relatives. It's conducted by a medicine man or another adult who'd been a Hunka. This ceremony provides a new family for a child who doesn't have a home."

"Did you and Mary do that?"

"No." She lifted her soda, took a sip, placed the can on the table. Walker's gaze followed her every move. She tried to avoid eye contact, but it didn't help. She could feel him looking at her. "In those days Mary wasn't connected to her heritage. She was defying tradition, isolating herself from the community. A Hunka ceremony would have been too Indian. Too Lakota."

"So she just kept you without adopting you?"

"Yes." Tamra tasted her soda again, wishing Walker would quit scrutinizing her. "We could do it now, though. People of any age can become Hunka if both parties agree."

"Don't," he said.

"Don't what? Have a ceremony?" Tired of his male dominance, she lifted her chin, challenging him. "That's not your choice to make."

"I don't want you to be her adopted daughter. I don't want to be related to you." He moved away from the dresser. "And I'm sure you know why."

Did she? She glanced at the bed, at the maroon

and blue quilt, at the plain white pillowcases. Then she looked at him. A bit woozy, she took a steadying breath. "Nothing's going to happen."

"Yes, it is. Sooner or later, we'll end up there."

There.

His bed.

She struggled to maintain her decorum, to seem unaffected. "That's awfully presumptuous of you."

He finished his drink, then grabbed the chair across from her. In one heart-stopping move, he spun it around and straddled it. "I'm not saying that I want it to happen. I'm just saying that it will."

Tamra felt as though she'd just been straddled. Ridden hard and put away…

…wet.

She moistened her lips. "I'm not going to sleep with you."

"Yes, you are." He didn't smile. He didn't flirt. But he shifted in his chair, bumping his fly against it. "We're going to tear off each other's clothes. And we're going to be sorry afterward, wondering what the hell we did."

"I don't have affairs. Not like that."

"Neither do I."

"Then why are we having this stupid conversation?"

"Because I couldn't stop thinking about you last night." He made a tense face. "And it's pissing me off."

She shook her head. He had to be the most difficult man she'd ever met. "Everything pisses you off, Walker."

He squinted at her. "Did you think about me last night?"

Her pulse tripped, stumbled like a clumsy little kid playing hopscotch in the rain. "No."

"Liar."

Yes, she thought. Liar, liar, pants on fire. But she'd be damned if she would admit it. She'd slept with the windows open, letting the breeze stir her hair, her half-naked body. "You're not my type."

"You're not mine, either." He paused, then checked her out, up and down, from head to toe. "But you're hot, sexy as sin. For an Indian," he added, making her scowl.

"I wouldn't go to bed with you if you were the last half-breed on earth."

He smiled at that. "Good. Then it won't happen. We're safe."

She was already safe. She'd been on the Pill since her baby girl died. Since she'd decided that she wasn't getting pregnant again. At least not by a man she wasn't married to.

Walker rocked in his chair, and she tried to think of something to say, something to wipe that cynical smile off his face. She certainly wasn't going to discuss birth control with him. She knew that wasn't the kind of safe he was referring to.

He was talking about their emotions, their feelings. Sex they would regret.

"What did my mother do with the money?" he asked, changing the topic so abruptly, she merely blinked at him.

"What?"

"The thirty grand. How'd she spend it?"

Tamra took a moment to gather her thoughts, to

compose her senses. "Maybe you should ask her about this."

"I'm asking you." He leaned back. "It's easier for me to talk to you. You're—" the cynical smile returned "—not as vulnerable."

He had no idea, she thought. He didn't have a clue. But how could he? She hadn't told him that she'd lost a child. That she understood his mother's pain. "Mary bought the mobile home we're living in. It was used, so it wasn't very expensive."

"So there was money left over?"

"Yes. And she invested that."

"Really?" He seemed surprised. "Were they sound investments?"

"Sound enough. There was enough to help me go to college."

"Damn." He dragged a hand through his sexually appealing hair, messing it up a little. "My mom sent her non-Hunka kid to college. Doesn't that beat all?"

"Beat all what?" Struggling to keep her cool, she blew an exasperated sigh. "I worked hard on my education. I earned a scholarship, too."

"To a tribal college?"

"To San Francisco State University."

He practically gaped at her. "You went to SFSU? You lived in California? Where I live?"

"That's right." She'd spent her entire childhood dreaming of bigger and better things. "And I brought Mary with me."

"Why San Francisco? Why did you choose a university there?"

"Because I knew Spencer had taken you and Charlotte to Northern California. And I wanted Mary to feel like she had a connection to her children, even if she was never going to see them." Tamra finished her soda and cursed her pounding heart. "So we rented a little apartment and tried to make a go of things. I got a part-time job and earned a degree in marketing, and Mary got a full-time job, working at a hospital. Later she became a certified nurse's aid."

He sat on the edge of the bed. "A marketing degree. And you came back to Pine Ridge?"

"Yes, we did."

"Why?"

"Why not? This is our home."

"Fine. Don't tell me the whole story. I don't care anyway."

But he did, she thought. Or he wouldn't be so hurt about Mary letting him go. "Have you called your sister yet? Did you tell Charlotte that you found your mom?"

"Yes." He made a face at the phone, cursing the object as if it were his enemy. "But she's not coming back to the States. Not for a little while. Can you believe it? She thinks I need to spend some time with Mary first. To get to know her."

"Sounds logical to me."

"Because you're a woman. Your kind stick together."

She couldn't help but smile. "I think I'm going to like your sister."

"I'm sure you will." He quit snarling at the phone

and noticed her smile. "Don't patronize me. I'm being serious."

"So am I." But she laughed in spite of herself. "You're just so agitated all the time, Walker. Everything upsets you."

"And you think that's funny?" He grabbed a pillow off the bed and threw it at her.

She caught it and tossed it back at him. Then they both fell silent.

"Want to get a pizza with me?" he asked suddenly.

Was he inviting her on a date? No, she thought, not after his spiel about their warped attraction. He was probably just bored, looking for something to do. "Sure, I guess. But on the rez. Not here. And I have to stop by a friend's house first."

"I noticed the pizza place at Pine Ridge. But I haven't eaten there."

"Don't worry. It won't make you sick."

He shrugged off her sarcasm. "It's a franchise I'm familiar with."

She came to her feet. "I'll drive. And on the way I'll teach you about Lakota protocol." She dug through her purse, snagged her keys. "Indian 101."

"I can hear it now. Don't point, Walker. And don't get drunk on the rez." He followed her out to her truck. "All those winos I saw must have missed your class."

Wiseguy, she thought. "Just listen and learn."

"Yes, ma'am."

He climbed in the passenger seat, and she gunned the engine, wondering what she'd just gotten herself into.

Three

Walker studied Tamra's profile. He had so many questions about her, about his mother. He was even curious about Lakota protocol. Although he wasn't sure why.

"Who told you I was looking for my mom?" he asked.

"I heard it through the moccasin telegraph. Someone who knew someone who knew someone else." She turned onto the highway. "You're lucky that Mary works at the PHS. That people are familiar with her. It's not easy to locate someone on the rez."

"No, I suppose not." Which was what he had been counting on. "Everything is so spread out."

She continued driving. By Walker's standard, her

pickup was old, an early-eighties model with plenty of mileage. But it seemed reliable enough. At least, he hoped so. He knew there were places in Indian Country where neither cell phones or CB radios worked. But for now they were still in Nebraska.

"Did you forget about my lesson?" he asked.

"No. I'm just deciding where to start."

He examined her profile again, thinking how striking she was. Her prominent cheekbones, the slight imperfection of her nose, the way her hair framed her face. Her eyes fascinated him, too. Whenever she looked at him, heat surged through his veins.

A sexual response, he thought. Lust in the first degree.

"We'll start with respectful eye contact," she said, making him blink, making him realize how closely he was watching her. "In the old way, you're supposed to avoid eye contact with your elders. And children were taught not to stare. When you stare at someone, you're challenging them."

He glanced away. He'd been staring at her from the moment they'd met. Of course, she'd done her fair share of locking gazes with him, too.

"As for pointing," she went on to say, "the Lakota gesture with their lips."

He frowned. "Their lips?"

"Like this?" She moved her mouth in his direction.

He tried it and made her laugh.

"You're overdoing it, Walker. You look like Mick Jagger."

He laughed, too. "What other social laws should

I know about?" he asked, deciding he enjoyed her company, her relaxed sense of humor.

"Addressing a family member by a kinship term is part of the old way."

"Like mother, son, daughter? That sort of thing?"

"Yes. But some of the terms are quite specific. Older brother. Younger sister. Male to female. Female to male."

He leaned back in his seat, knowing this would be important to Charlotte. "What's the term for younger sister?"

"From a male to a female? *Tanksi,* I think. Sometimes I get confused. I'm still learning the language."

Walker nodded. He suspected that Mary hadn't raised Tamra in a traditional manner. Not after the things she'd said about his mother avoiding the Hunka and other Lakota ceremonies. "Does my mom speak the language?"

"She's not fluent, but she's working on it. We're both trying to make up for the past. For the years we didn't embrace our culture." She kept her hands on the steering wheel. "But we're still not overly traditional. We just do the best we can, trying to respect others."

Walker tried to picture Tamra in San Francisco, far away from the Lakota. Knowing that she'd chosen SFSU because of him and Charlotte made him feel closer to her. But it made him uncomfortable, too. She'd grown up in his shadow, and now he was struggling to survive in hers.

"Are their different types of Sioux?" he asked,

still trying to absorb his culture. "Or are they all Lakota?"

"There are three branches," she responded. "Lakota, Dakota and Nakota, who are also called the Yankton Sioux."

"So where does Oglala come into it?"

"It's one of the seven Lakota bands. It means 'they scatter their own' or 'dust scatters.'" She sent him a half-cocked smile. "But the Oglala have seven bands of their own, too."

"Okay, now you're confusing me." He shook his head and laughed. "So much for Indian 101. This is turning into an advanced course."

She laughed, too. "It's not as complicated as it sounds."

"If you say so." He glanced out the window and noticed they were on the reservation, heading toward the town of Pine Ridge. He recognized the road.

"What kind of work do you do?" he asked. "What keeps you busy around here?"

"I'm the director of volunteer services for a local nonprofit organization. We supply food and clothing to people on the reservation."

He raised his eyebrows. "An Indian charity?" Was that the extent of her life? Everything Lakota?

"It's important," she countered. "It's meaningful."

"Yes, but being the director of volunteer services doesn't require a marketing degree. Sounds like a waste of your college years to me."

She gave him a quick, sharp look. "I coordinate media events, too."

Small-time stuff, he imagined.

By the time they arrived in downtown Pine Ridge, tension buzzed between them. So much for enjoying her company, he thought. For her easy sense of humor. But he supposed it was his fault. He'd criticized her job.

He considered apologizing, then decided that would be dishonest. Her education wasn't being utilized, not to its full potential. She'd cheated herself by coming back to the reservation, by living on her homeland.

The town of Pine Ridge had one traffic light and four water towers. There was plenty of activity, generated from the Billy Mills Auditorium, tribal offices and the Oglala Department of Public Safety, but Walker noticed that a lot of people were doing nothing, just sitting on a bench, talking away their boredom.

Tamra stopped for gas at Big Bat's, a convenience store, eatery and gathering place for locals. He'd heard it was Lakota owned and operated, unlike some of the businesses on Pine Ridge. He had to admit it was impressive, something he hadn't expected when he'd first arrived. But even so, he hadn't been inclined to hang out there.

The pizza place was in town, too. As well as a taco stand and a market.

"Are you still interested in having pizza with me?" he asked, as they left the gas station. "Or did I blow it?"

"I'll eat with you. But after we go by my friend's house, remember?"

Yeah, he remembered. "Is this a traditional friend? An elder? Should I avoid eye contact?"

"Michele is the same age as me. We went to high school together, and she won't care if you stare at her. She'll probably like it."

A smile twitched his lips. "The way you do?"

"I never said that."

"You didn't have to."

She ignored his last comment, so they drove in silence, past empty fields and into a hodge-podge of unattractive houses.

"So what's the deal with Michele?" he wanted to know. "Why are we visiting her?"

"I'm loaning her some money. Her daughter's birthday is coming up, and she's short right now."

He looked out the window, saw sporadic rows of wire fences, garments hanging on outdated clotheslines. "Is she on welfare?"

"She's a single mom. And, yes, she receives Aid to Dependent Children." Tamra's truck rattled on the roughly paved road. "Does it matter?"

"I just wondered." He couldn't imagine not having any money for your child's birthday. But he knew his parents had been destitute at the time his dad died. If he looked deep within himself, he could recall the shame it had caused him, the feeling of despair.

For Walker there had been nothing worse than being poor.

Michele's house was a pale-blue structure with a set of worn-out steps leading to the front door. It was, Walker thought, a stark contrast to the diversity of the land. The grassy plains, rolling hills, buttes and mesas. The beauty he'd refused to appreciate.

A little girl, maybe three or four years old, sat on the steps, with a loyal dog, a mutt of some kind, snuggled beside her.

Although a group of older kids played in the yard, he sensed she was the upcoming birthday girl.

"How many kids does Michele have?" he asked Tamra, as she parked her truck in a narrow driveway.

"Just one. The rest are her nieces and nephews."

Walker watched them run through the grass, tagging each other with laughter and adolescent squeals. "Do they all live here?"

She nodded. "Along with their parents. There's a shortage of houses on the reservation. They don't have anywhere else to go."

He thought about his trilevel condo, the sprawling rooms with French doors and leaded-glass windows. The redwood deck and private hot tub. The enormous kitchen he rarely used.

He ran his hand through his hair, smoothing it away from his face, trying to shed the sudden guilt of having money. "That's a lot of people in one house."

"It's a common situation."

"How common?"

"The Tribal Housing Authority is trying to provide homes, but they have a waiting list of at least twelve hundred people. It's been like that for a long time." She turned to look at him. "When I was growing up, before Mary took us in, my mom and I drifted, trying to find a permanent place to stay. In the summer we camped out, but in the winter we had to find some sort of roof over our heads."

He pictured her as a little girl, living like a half-starved gypsy. "Why are these houses so close together and my mom's by itself?"

"Mary lives on her family's land allotment, which is what most families did in the old days. They had log cabins, with gardens and animals." She sighed, her voice fading into the stillness of her truck. "But as time passed, it became increasingly difficult for people to remain on their land allotments. They couldn't afford to improve their homes, to stay in the country with no running water or electricity. And some families lost their land altogether, so they had to move into government projects."

"Like this?"

She nodded. "It's called cluster housing. It was instituted in the 1960s to provide modern conveniences. But the lack of economic infrastructure created reservation ghettos." Tamra reached for her purse. "Cluster housing is only a portion of the problem. There are families who still don't have electricity or running water. People staying in abandoned shacks or old trailers. Or camping out or living in their cars, the way my mom and I did."

He couldn't think of an appropriate response. He'd witnessed the poverty, seen signs of it all over the reservation, but until now he hadn't let it touch him.

They exited the vehicle, and Tamra called out to the older kids. They grinned and waved at her. Walker wondered why they seemed so happy, so lighthearted and free. He could barely breathe.

The little girl on the steps grinned, too. She wore a pink top, denim shorts and a couple of minor scrapes on her knees. Brownish-black hair fell in a single braid, neatly plaited and shining in the July sun. Her feet, dusted with soil from the earth, were devoid of shoes.

When Tamra sat next to her, the child wiggled with familiarity. The dog got excited, too, slapping his tail against the splintered wood. Was the mutt a stray? A hungry soul Michele's abundant family had taken pity on?

Walker moved closer and crouched down. Tamra told him the girl's name was Maya. A bit shy, she banged her knobby knees together, ducked her head and gave him a sweet hello.

He wanted to scoop her up and take her home, spoil her with clothes and toys and fancy ribbons for her hair.

But at this point he wanted to take Tamra home, as well. He envisioned spoiling her, too, making up for her past, for the hardship she'd endured.

As she turned to look at him, he considered kissing her. Just a soft kiss, he thought. Something that wouldn't alarm the child.

The front door flew open, and Walker's heart jackhammered its way to his throat. Romancing Tamra was a crazy notion. They'd already agreed they weren't going to sleep together.

A young, full-figured woman came out of the

house and greeted Tamra. Like most of the people on the rez, she had distinct sound to her voice—a flat tone, an accent Walker was still getting used to.

"Why are you sitting on the stoop?" she asked. "Why didn't you come in?"

"We wanted to visit with Maya first," Tamra told her, rising so they could hug. A second later she introduced Walker.

But the other woman, the infamous Michele, had already taken a keen interest in him. He shook her hand, and she flashed a smile that broadened her moon-shaped face.

"Where did Tamra find you?" She tossed a glance at her friend. "You show up with this yummy *iyeska* and leave me in the dark?"

Yummy *iyeska?*

It was better than being a stupid one, Walker supposed. But since that Lakota word still eluded him, he wasn't sure how to react.

Tamra didn't react, either. "He's Mary's son."

"No shi—" Michele started to cuss, then caught herself. Her little girl was watching the adults like a fledging hawk.

Dark eyes. Rapt attention.

"So you're the boy who was stolen by that mean *wasicu,*" Michele said to Walker.

He tried not to frown, to let his emotions show. *Wasicu.* White man, he thought. That was easy enough to translate. "Uncle Spencer raised my sister and me."

Michele stuffed her hands into the pockets of threadbare jeans. "Well, it's good to have you here."

"Thanks." He glanced at the kids playing in the grass, then at Maya, who still sat on the steps with the big mangy dog. "I live in San Francisco. And I'll be going home in a few weeks."

"Too bad." Michele bumped Tamra's shoulder. "*Ennit,* friend?"

Tamra nodded, then made eye contact with Walker. But he knew she wasn't challenging him. It was a look of confusion, of an attraction that was sure to go awry.

Michele guided Walker and Tamra into the house, looping her arms through theirs. Maya popped up and followed them. In no time the other kids came inside, too, joining their parents, who gathered around a TV set with snowy reception.

Two of the older women bounded into the kitchen and began preparing a snack of some kind. Walker hadn't expected them to cook for him. With all the mouths they had to feed, he felt awkward about being fussed over. But he appeared to be an honored guest.

Mary Little Dove's son.

Maya warmed up to him, sitting beside him in a tired old chair. He moved over to accommodate her, and the lopsided cushion sagged under his weight, making him even more aware of his run-down surroundings. The faded brown carpet was worn to the bone, and sleeping mats were stacked in every corner.

He glanced across the crowded room and noticed the exchange of a twenty-dollar bill going from Tamra to Michele. The birthday loan. Walker tipped bellmen at hotels more than that.

He thought about the stocks Spencer had willed to him. Was it blood money? Payment in full? Or was he just lucky that his uncle had given a damn about him?

The Ashton patriarch. The mean *wasicu.*

The snack was a platter of fry bread, a staple among most Indian tribes, accompanied by bowls of *wojapi,* a Lakota pudding made with blueberries, water, sugar and flour.

Following young Maya's lead, Walker dipped a piece of fry bread into the *wojapi* and realized he was surrounded by people who seemed genuinely interested in him. Still seated in the sagging chair, with Maya by his side, he talked and laughed with Tamra's friends.

And for a few surprisingly stress-free hours, he actually enjoyed being in Pine Ridge.

The sun had begun to set, disappearing behind the hills, painting the sky in majestic colors.

For Tamra, this was home. The land, the trees, the tranquility. The impoverished reservation. A place she used to hate. But she would never hate it again. She knew better now.

Maka Ina, she thought. Mother Earth.

She glanced at Walker. He sat next to her, watching the horizon. They occupied a rustic porch swing at his mom's house that complained every so often, the wood creaking from age.

He hadn't said much since they'd left Michele's house, but he seemed reflective.

Sticking to their original plan, they'd gotten a pepperoni pizza. But instead of eating it, they'd put it in the fridge, saving it for later, waiting for Mary to come home from work. But for now, their bellies were still full of fry bread and *wojapi*.

"What's an *iyeska?*" Walker asked.

"A half-breed."

"That's it? That's all it means?"

"Yes. Do you want me to translate yummy, too?"

He smiled, just little enough to send her heart into a girlish patter.

When his smile faded, she sensed the hurt inside him, the pain that often came with being a mixed blood. "Michele wasn't trying to insult you."

He gazed into the distance, at the land of his ancestors. Tamra waited for him to respond. Somewhere nearby, birds chirped, preparing for their evening roost.

"I know Michele wasn't putting me down," he said. "But the first day I arrived, a wino called me a stupid *iyeska*. It never occurred me that it meant half-breed. In San Francisco, people think I'm this major Indian. No matter how much I downplay my heritage, they still notice, still comment on it. But here I'm not Indian enough."

"It's the way you carry yourself, Walker."

He shifted on the swing, scraping his lace-up boots on the porch. He wore comfortable-looking khakis and a casual yet trendy shirt. A strand of his hair fell across his forehead, masking one of his eyebrows. "What's that supposed to mean?"

"There's always been dissention between the full

bloods and the mixed bloods on the reservation." A war she understood all too well. "But sometimes *iyeska* refers to someone's attitude, not his or her blood quantum. Full bloods can be *iyeskas,* too. Indians who think white."

Edgy as ever, he frowned at her. "Fine. Then that's what I am."

"You didn't seem like an *iyeska* once you got to know Michele's family. You seemed like a full blood."

"I did?" He smoothed his hair, dragging the loose strand away from his forehead. Then he laughed a little. "I really liked Michele's family, but they weren't totally traditional. I don't know if I could handle that." He released a rough breath. "I'm too set in my *wasicu* ways."

"Maybe so." She grinned at him. "But you're starting to speak Lakota."

He grinned, too. "A few words. My uncle is probably rolling over in his grave."

For a moment she thought his good mood would falter. That his grave-rolling uncle would sour his smile. But he managed to hold on, even if she saw a deeply rooted ache in his eyes.

"What does *ennit* mean?" he asked.

"It's not a Lakota word. It's an interjection a lot of Indians use. *Ennit?* instead of *isn't it?*"

"You don't say it."

"I've never been partial to slang."

"Thank God," he said, and made her laugh.

She looked up at the sky and noticed the sun was

gone. Dusk had fallen, like a velvet curtain draping the hills. Beside her, Walker fell silent. She suspected he was enjoying the scenery, too. The pine-scented air, the summer magic.

He interrupted her thoughts. "I almost kissed you earlier."

Her lungs expanded, her heart went haywire. Fidgeting with the hem on her blouse, she tried to think of something to say. But the words stuck in her throat.

"Did you hear me?"

"Yes." Beneath her plain white bra, her nipples turned hard—hard enough to graze her top, to make bulletlike impressions.

"Would you have kissed me back?"

"No," she lied, crossing her arms, trying to hide her breasts.

"I think you would've," he said.

Tamra forced herself to look at him. A mistake, she realized. An error in judgment. Now her panties were warm, the cotton sticking to her skin. "We're supposed to get past this."

"Past what?" He leaned into her, so close, his face was only inches from hers. "Wanting each other?"

She nodded, and he touched her cheek. A gentle caress. A prelude to a kiss.

She waited. But he didn't do it.

He dropped his hand to his lap and moved back, away from her. "We are." He brushed his own fly, tensed his fingers and made a frustrated fist. "We're past it."

She stole a glance at his zipper, looked away, hoped to God she wasn't blushing. "Then let's talk about something else."

"Fine. But I can't think of anything." He spread his thighs, slouching a little. "Can you?"

"Not really, no." And his posture was making her dizzy, ridiculously light-headed. She could almost imagine sliding between his legs, whispering naughty things in his ear.

He cleared his throat. "How about San Francisco?"

She fussed with her blouse again. "What?"

"We can discuss San Francisco."

"You want to compare notes?" She told herself to relax, to quit behaving like a crush-crazed teenager. "About what? Our alma mater?"

He shook his head. "I went to UC Berkeley."

"Then what?"

"I want to know what happened in San Francisco. Why you didn't stay there." A slight breeze blew, cooling the prairie, stirring the air.

She squinted, saw a speckling of stars, milky dots that had yet to shine.

"Will you tell me?" he asked.

"Yes," she said, drawing the strength to talk about her baby, the infant she'd buried in Walker's hometown.

Four

Tamra took a deep breath, fighting the pain that came with the past. Walker didn't say anything. He just waited for her to speak.

"I had a baby in San Francisco," she said. "A little girl. But she was stillborn."

"Oh, God. I'm sorry. I had no idea." He reached over to take her hand, to skim his fingers across hers.

She closed her eyes for a moment, grateful for his touch, his compassion. "She's still there. In a cemetery near my old apartment."

"Do you want me to visit her when I go home?" he asked. "To take her some flowers?"

Tamra opened her eyes, felt her heart catch in her throat. She hadn't expected him to make such a kind offer. "That would mean a lot to me. Sometimes I worry that she's lonely, all by herself in a big city. I know that's a crazy way to feel, but I can't help it." She looked up at the sky again. "I should have buried her here. But at the time, I was determined to stay in San Francisco, to prove I could make it."

"But you changed your mind?"

She nodded. "After a while, I realized I was spinning in circles. Mourning my baby and trying to be someone I wasn't." She looked at him, saw him looking back at her. "Mary and I went to San Francisco because we were defying our heritage, because we wanted to be white. But we're not. We're Lakota. And this is our home."

He released her hand, but he did it gently, slowly. "What about your baby's father? How does he fit into all of this?"

"He doesn't, not anymore."

"But he did. He gave you a child."

When her chest turned tight, she blew out the breath she was holding. "He broke up with me when he found out I was pregnant. He wasn't her father. He was a sperm donor."

Walker searched her gaze. "Did you love him?"

"Yes." She shifted in her seat, causing the swing to rock. "His name is Edward Louis. I met him through JT Marketing, the firm I worked for. He's one of their top clients."

"A white guy?"

"Yes. A corporate mogul. The president of a wheel corporation. You know, fancy rims and tires."

"I'm sorry he hurt you." Walker paused, frowned. "Is it Titan Motorsports? Is that the company he represents?"

"No. Why? Does it matter?"

"I have Titan wheels on my Jag. I just wanted to be sure I wasn't supporting the enemy."

She smiled, leaned against his shoulder, decided she liked him. "Your Jaguar is safe."

"Good." He leaned against her, too. "I don't understand how a man could leave a woman who's carrying his child."

"He thought I trapped him. That I got pregnant on purpose. He didn't love me the way I loved him. But I'm not blaming that on his race. It doesn't have anything to do with him being white. Plenty of Indian men walk away, too."

"Like your dad?"

"Exactly."

"I'm still having a hard time with my mom," Walker said. "It bothers me that she didn't fight to keep her children. That she let us go. But on the other hand, I'm grateful that I've lived a privileged life. That I wasn't raised here." He made a face. "I realize how awful that sounds, but I can't help it. It's just so damn poor."

"That was part of Mary's reasoning, I think. Why she didn't fight. Why she let Spencer take you."

"So it was more than him just threatening her?"

Tamra nodded. "It was the hopelessness she felt, the fear of not being able to provide for you and Charlotte. Eighty-five percent of the people on Pine

Ridge are unemployed. There's no industry, technology or commercial advancement to provide jobs."

"She has a job now."

"Twenty-two years after she let you and your sister go. Mary has come a long way since then."

"But Pine Ridge hasn't."

"Maybe not, but we keep trying. Mary knows she was wrong. That she should have fought to keep her kids. We have to believe in ourselves, to teach our young to battle the hopelessness, to rise above it."

"That's a noble concept. But how realistic is it?"

"Come to work with me tomorrow and find out."

He raised his eyebrows. "Is that a dare?"

"You bet it is." She wasn't about to let him leave the reservation on a discouraging note. She wanted him to be proud of his birthright.

"Then what choice do I have?" He gave her a playful nudge. "I'm not the kind of man who backs away from a challenge. Especially from a pretty girl."

She didn't flirt back. At least not in a lighthearted way. She was too emotional to goof around, too serious to make silly jokes. In the waning light, she touched the side of his face, absorbing the texture of his skin.

His chest rose and fell, his breathing rough, a little anxious. "Being nice to me is going to get you into trouble, Tamra."

"Maybe. But you've been nice to me tonight. You offered to visit my baby. To bring her flowers."

"What was her name?" he asked.

"Jade."

"Like the stone?"

"When I was pregnant, Mary bought me a figurine for my birthday. A jade turtle that fit in the palm of my hand. It was my protector."

"Do you still have it?"

She shook her head. "I buried it with my baby. I gave it to her."

He leaned forward. "Jade was lucky to have you."

She tried not to cry, but her eyes betrayed her. They burned with the threat of tears, with the memory of her daughter, with the little kicks and jabs that had glorified her womb. "I wanted her so badly. But toward the end, I knew something was wrong. She wasn't moving inside me anymore."

"I'm so sorry." He touched her face, the way she'd grazed his. And then he brushed his lips across hers. A feathery kiss, a warm embrace.

Desperate for his compassion, she slid her arms around his neck and drew him closer. His tongue touched hers, and she welcomed the sensation, the slow, sensual comfort of his mouth.

He tasted like blueberries, like Lakota pudding. Masculine heat, drenched in sugar. She couldn't seem to get enough. Desperate for more, she deepened the kiss.

And then a car sounded, moving along the road, coming toward the house.

Like kids who'd gotten caught with their pants down, they jerked apart.

"My mother's home." He grabbed the chain on the swing, trying to keep it from rattling, from making too much noise. "I guess we should reheat the pizza."

"Yes, of course." Tamra stood, smoothed her blouse, wondered if Walker's prediction would come true. That they would, indeed, end up in bed.

And be sorry about it afterward.

Walker, Tamra and Mary sat in the living room, the coffee table littered with napkins, sodas and left-over pizza. They'd eaten their meal, and now they battled a round of silence.

Walker wondered what Tamra was thinking, if she was as confused as he was. With each passing hour, he became more and more protective of her. Not that he was happy about it. In some ways, arguing with her was easier. But he wasn't about to pick a fight.

If anything, he should cut his trip short and go home. But he knew he wouldn't. Not until he figured out what to do about Tamra. If he walked away too soon, he would feel like a coward.

"Would you like to spend the night here?" his mother asked, catching him off guard.

He reached for his drink and took a hard, cold swig. Sleep under the same roof as Tamra? Was his mother daft? Couldn't she see what was happening? "I don't think that's a good idea."

"Why not?"

Because I want to have sex with your non-Hunka daughter, he thought. "Because I don't have anything with me. All of my stuff is at the motel. My rental car, too."

"Then how about tomorrow night?" Mary gave him a beseeching look. "It's been so many years since I've had my boy with me. I just hate to let you go."

Guilt clawed at his conscience. He hadn't come to Pine Ridge to get hot and bothered over Tamra. He'd arrived in South Dakota to search for his mother. And now that he'd found her, he hadn't given her the time or the consideration she deserved. He hadn't given her a chance.

"Sure," he said. "I can stay tomorrow."

"And the next night after that?" she pressed, her voice much too hopeful.

He nodded, feeling kind of loopy inside. Walker wasn't used to maternal affection. Spencer's wife, Lilah, had all but ignored him, especially when he was young.

Of course, he'd been too enamored of Spencer to worry about getting attention from Lilah. Besides, he'd always seen her as a tragic character, lost in a socialite world, a place with no substance. And from what he'd observed, she wasn't the greatest mother to her own kids. So why would she treat him or his sister with care?

He'd survived without a mom, something he'd gotten used to. And now here he was, sitting next to Mary on her plain blue sofa, with boyish butterflies in his stomach.

The longing in her eyes made him ill at ease. Yet somewhere in the cavern of his lost memories, in the depth of his eight-year-old soul, he appreciated it. He just wished he could return the favor. But as it was, she still seemed like a stranger.

"Walker is coming to work with me tomorrow," Tamra said, drawing his attention. "So he should probably drive his car over in the morning."

"That's a great idea," Mary put in.

Yeah, great. He was being prodded by two decision-making females. He addressed Tamra. "You still have to take me back to the motel tonight."

She chewed her bottom lip. "I know."

Curious, he gauged her reaction. Was she wondering if he would kiss her again? If once they were alone, they would pick up where they'd left off?

Well, they wouldn't, he concluded. He was going to keep his hands to himself, control his urges, even if it killed him. What good would it do to pursue a relationship with her? To get tangled up in an affair? He was the up-and-coming CEO of a company that had been his life's blood, and she was dedicated to her reservation, to a place that would never fit his fast-paced, high-finance lifestyle. One or two heartfelt moments on Pine Ridge wouldn't change him. He would always be an *iyeska*. And he would always be connected to Uncle Spencer—the tough, ruthless man who'd raised him.

"Do you want to see some old family photos?" Mary asked.

Walker glanced up, realizing he'd zoned out, gotten lost in troubled thoughts. "I'm sorry. What?"

"Pictures of you and Charlotte when you were little," she said. "They were the first things I packed. After I was released from the hospital, Spencer told me to grab a few belongings and he would send the rest. But I didn't trust him, so I took mementos I didn't want him to destroy."

His lungs constricted. "Sure. Okay. I'd like to see the pictures."

Mary smiled, her dark eyes turning bright. "I'll get them." She rose from the sofa. "I'll be right back."

After she left the room, he locked gazes with Tamra, who sat across from him in a faded easy chair. The golden hue from a nearby lamp sent shadows across her face, making her look soft, almost ghostly.

A Lakota spirit.

He rubbed his arm, fighting an instant chill. Suddenly he could hear voices in his head, the cry of a woman and a child being gunned down, running from the cavalry, falling to the frozen earth. A play-acted scene from an Indian documentary he'd caught on the History Channel a few months ago.

"What's wrong?" Tamra asked.

"Nothing."

"You're frowning."

He tried to relax his forehead. "It's not intentional."

"Here they are." Mary returned with two large photo albums.

Walker broke eye contact with Tamra, thinking about the baby she'd buried, the child he'd assumed responsibility for. Flowers on a grave.

His mother resumed her seat, handing him the first album. He opened the cover, then nearly lost his breath.

"That's your father and me on our wedding day. It wasn't a fancy ceremony. We went to the justice of the peace."

"You look just like Charlotte, the way she looks now." Stunned, he studied the picture. He hadn't noticed the resemblance until now, hadn't realized how much his sister had taken after Mary. But then, his mother had aged harshly, the years taking their toll.

"Really? Oh, my." She seemed pleased, thrilled that her daughter had grown up in her image. Especially since Charlotte had called Mary earlier, promising that she would return to the States next week. They'd talked easily, almost as if they'd never been apart.

Walker had been a tad envious, wondering how his sister had managed to carry on a conversation like that. Within a few a minutes she'd accomplished more than he had in two full days.

And over the phone, no less.

Mary turned the page. "Here you are. On the day you were born. Look at that sweet little face."

Sweet? He wasn't an authority on newborns, but he wasn't impressed with what he saw. "I look like a prune." A dried plum, he thought, with a cap of dark hair.

When his mom swatted his shoulder, he scrunched up his features, mocking the picture.

And then suddenly he felt sad. He noticed Tamra, sitting alone in her chair, ghostlike once again.

Was she thinking about Jade?

Trying to hide her emotions, she gave him a brave smile. But it was too late. He was already affected by her, already wishing he could hold her, take away her pain.

Too many lost children, he thought. Too much

heartache. Now his mother was watching him with anticipation, waiting for him to look at the next picture.

To remember his youth.

But the only thing that came to mind was the documentary he recalled on TV. The woman and her child stumbling to the ground. A depiction of someone's ancestors.

Bleeding in the snow.

Walker rode shotgun in Tamra's truck, traveling from Rapid City, South Dakota, back to the reservation. They'd spent the morning in Rapid City, where she'd given him a tour of the warehouse that stocked food donations. The Oyate Project, the nonprofit organization she worked for, was a small but stable operation. She claimed there were bigger charities in the area, but she'd been involved in the Oyate Project since its inception.

Oyate, Walker had learned, meant "the People" in Lakota. Her people, his people, she'd told him.

He glanced out his window and saw a vast amount of nothingness—grassy fields, dry brush, a horizon that went on forever. Rapid City was about 120 miles from Pine Ridge, a long and seemingly endless drive and they were only halfway through it.

"So this is the route your delivery trucks take?" he asked.

"Yes, but because of the distance, the weather can vary, particularly in the winter. Sometimes a truck leaves Rapid City, where it's sixty degrees and hits the reservation in the middle of a whiteout."

"A blizzard?"

She nodded, and he pictured the land blanketed in snow. "Some of the homes aren't accessible during heavy snows or rain, are they?"

"No, they're not. We try to provide propane fuel and heating stoves. We haul firewood, too. But there are so many people to reach, so many families who need to keep warm."

He thought about the years Tamra and her mother had spent dodging the cold. "Do you have any extended family? Anyone who's still alive?"

"I have some distant cousins on my dad's side, but we don't socialize much. They tend to party, drink too much." She heaved a heavy-hearted sigh. "I've tried to help them get sober, but they shoo me away. They think I'm a do-gooder."

"No one could say that about me," he admitted.

"You've never offered to help anyone?"

"Not firsthand. I send checks to charities, but I've always thought of them as tax write-offs. I don't get emotionally involved."

She slanted him a sideways glance. "You will today."

He tried to snare her gaze, but she'd already turned back to the road. "So where exactly are we going?"

"To meet one of the trucks at a drop-off location. It's my home base, where my office is."

They arrived about forty-five minutes later. The drop-off location was a prefab building equipped with garage-style doors. A group of cars were parked around the structure, where volunteers waited for the delivery truck.

Michele and her daughter, Maya, were among the volunteers, ready to help those less fortunate than themselves. Walker was impressed. Michele was living in an overcrowded home, trying to make ends meet, yet she was willing to drive her beat-up car to other communities on the rez, delivering food to hungry families. He suspected the Oyate Project was paying for her gas, but she was offering her time, her heart, for free.

She greeted him and Tamra with a hug. Maya looked up at them and grinned. Soon another volunteer engaged Tamra in a conversation and she excused herself, leaving Walker with Michele and her sweet little girl.

As casually as possible he removed some cash from his wallet and slipped it into Michele's hand.

She gave him a confused look.

"For Maya's birthday," he said, as the child played in the dirt, drawing pictures with a stick.

Michele thanked him, giving him another hug, putting her mouth close to his ear. "I hope you hook up with my friend. She needs a guy like you."

He stepped back, felt his pulse stray. "I'm not hooking up with anybody."

"You sure about that?"

Was he? "I'm trying to be." He'd been doing his damnedest not to touch Tamra, not to kiss her again.

Michele angled her head. Her long, straight hair was clipped with a big, plastic barrette, and a bright blue T-shirt clung to her plus-size figure. "Maybe you shouldn't fight it."

He shifted his feet. They stood in the heat, with the sun beating down on their backs. "It would never work. I live in California."

"Yeah, but you're here now." She gave him a serious study. "And my friend is getting to you."

So he was supposed to live for the moment? Make a move on Tamra? Have a wham-bam-thank-you-ma'am with a woman who'd been through hell and back? Somehow he doubted that was what Michele had in mind. "You think I'll stay. You think that if I hook up with her, I'll make this place my home."

"Stranger things have happened."

Not that strange, he thought.

Tamra returned and invited him into her office. He entered the building with her, eager to escape. As much as he liked Michele, he didn't need to get side-tracked by her hope-filled notions.

Determined to keep his distance, he refrained from getting too close to Tamra. But once they were in her office with the door closed, he didn't have a choice. Her workspace put them in a confined area: a standard desk, a narrow bookcase, a file cabinet that took up way too much room.

She dug through the top drawer, removed a folder and sorted through it, gathering the papers she needed. Walker took a deep breath, and her fragrance accosted him like a floral-scented bandit. If he moved forward, just a little, just three or four small steps, he could take her in his arms.

Damn the consequences and kiss her.

The phone on her desk rang, jarring him back to reality.

She answered the call, and he cursed Michele for messing with his mind, for encouraging him to be with Tamra. Walker hadn't gotten laid in months. Of course, he knew Michele was talking about more than just sex.

"Are you ready?" Tamra asked.

He simply looked at her. He hadn't even realized that she'd hung up the phone. He'd been too busy feeling sorry for his neglected libido. "Ready for what?"

"To go back outside. Or would you rather wait here?"

"For what?"

"The truck." She made a curious expression. "Are you all right, Walker?"

A bit defensive, he frowned at her. "Why wouldn't I be?"

"How would I know? You're acting weird."

Did she have to be so pretty? So smooth and sultry? She wore jeans and an Oyate Project T-shirt, but it could have been a nightgown, a breezy fabric, an erotic temptation. "Maybe I'm just sick of the reservation."

She crossed her arms. "Then go home."

He didn't want to return to California, not without putting his hands all over her first. "I didn't mean it like that." Anxious, he leaned against the file cabinet. "And I don't want to fight with you."

"Me, neither."

She sighed, and he almost touched her.

Almost.

He decided it was safer waiting outside, even if Michele would probably be dogging his heels, giving him conspiratorial glances.

But luckily that didn't happen. The truck arrived, and the pace picked up. So much so, Walker got absorbed in the activity, helping the driver unload the food.

After the cartons were sorted and stacked, Tamra organized the volunteers and individual cars were packed with bags of perishable items and boxes of dry goods. Walker loaded the back of Tamra's vehicle with groceries from a checklist she'd given him.

Soon they were rolling across the plains again, heading to their first destination. He turned to look at her, knowing she was right. He was getting emotionally involved today. But not only with her charity.

He was getting attached to her, too.

Five

Walker and Tamra had spent the afternoon with families who had no electricity and no running water. People living in abandoned camper shells, in old shacks, in rusted-out trailers. But even so, he'd seen pride in their eyes, determination, kindness, a sense of community.

And now Tamra had taken him to the Wounded Knee Memorial. He wasn't sure why she'd decided to come here, especially today, after driving all over the reservation. They were both road weary and tired.

Walker studied his surroundings. Aside from a Lakota couple selling dream catchers in a shelter of pine boughs, there was no one around. He suspected a few tourists trickled by now and then, or else the enterprising young couple wouldn't have any customers.

A green sign, suffering from vandalism, offered a historical account of the Massacre of Wounded Knee. The word *massacre* had been bolted onto the sign with a sheet of metal, covering something below it.

"What did it say before?" Walker asked Tamra, who stood beside him, her hair glistening in the late-day sun.

"Battle," she told him.

"The Battle of Wounded Knee?"

"That was what the government originally called it."

But it wasn't a battle, Tamra explained, as he gazed at the sign. It was a massacre—a place where more than three hundred Indians, mostly women and children, were killed on December 29, 1890, for supporting the Ghost Dance, a religion that had been outlawed on Lakota reservations.

Fourteen days prior to the massacre, the tribal police murdered Sitting Bull at his home. That prompted Big Foot, another Lakota chief, to lead his band to Pine Ridge, where he hoped to seek shelter with Chief Red Cloud, who was trying to make peace with the army. But Big Foot, an old man ill with pneumonia, and most of his people, were exterminated instead. Those who survived told their story, recounting the chilling details.

"It was the Seventh Cavalry who shot them," Tamra said. "Custer's old unit. The government sent them, along with other troops, to arrest the Ghost Dancers. The morning after Big Foot and his band were captured, a gun went off during a scuffle. And that was it. That was how the massacre started." She paused, her voice impassioned with the past, with a war-torn history. "At first the struggle was fought at close quarters, but most of the Indians had already surrendered their weapons. There were only a hundred warriors. The rest were women, children and old men. When they ran to take cover, the cavalry opened fire with cannons that were positioned above the camp. Later some of the women were found two or three miles away, a sign that they were chased down and killed."

Walker glanced at the craft booth, where dream catchers fluttered, feathers stirring in the breeze. "The Seventh Cavalry got their revenge."

"Yes, they did." Tamra followed his gaze. "The Ghost Dance was supposed to bring back the old way, to encourage spiritual powers to save us. At the time, the government was reducing our land and cutting our promised rations. The Lakota were sick and starving. They needed hope."

"They needed the Ghost Dance," he said.

She nodded, and he thought about the documentary on TV, the reenactment of a woman and child bleeding in the snow. Was that a depiction of Wounded Knee? Of the massacre? He'd only caught a glimpse of it while he was switching channels, but it had affected him just the same.

"Someone found a baby still suckling from its dead mother," she said, her words creating a devastating image in his mind. "And after most of the people had been killed, there were soldiers who called out, claiming that those who weren't wounded should come forth, that they would be safe. But when some of the little boys crept out of their hiding places, they were butchered." She paused, took a breath. "We have an annual event called Future Generations Riders, where the organizers take a group of horseback riders, mostly children, on the same trail as the Wounded Knee victims. Sitting Bull's great-great-great-grandson is one of the leaders. Some of the kids don't know their culture, so it helps them learn, to look to the future. Hope can come from grief. From accepting who you are."

"Spencer told me that being Indian didn't matter," Walker admitted. "That I needed to forget about it if I wanted to succeed."

"I was told the same thing. From my mother, from your mother. But Mary and I have changed. We believe differently now."

"Can we visit the grave site?" he asked, compelled by his heritage, the Lakota blood he'd fought so hard to ignore.

"Yes, of course," she told him, meeting his gaze.

He wondered if she could see into his heart, if she knew what he was thinking. If she did, she didn't say anything. Instead she led him to a road that looped around like a teardrop.

On top of a hill, a rustic archway announced the entrance to the cemetery. A mass grave, hedged by a small slab of concrete, was marked with a stone obelisk, listing the names of the Indians buried there. Native gifts, feathers and tobacco offerings adorned their resting place. Surrounding the memorial were other graves, a bit more modern, scattered in the rough grass.

Walker reached for Tamra's hand and whispered a prayer. She slid her fingers through his, and they stood side by side, a man and a woman who'd forged a bond.

A closeness neither of them could deny.

After they went back to her truck, they sat in silence for a while. Finally he turned to look at her. She moved closer, and they kissed.

Slowly, gently.

And even though the exchange was more emotional than physical, more sweet than sexual, he wished they could make love tonight, hold each other in the same bed. Of course, he knew that wasn't possible. Especially since he'd agreed to stay at his mother's house.

Confused, he ended the kiss, still tasting her on his tongue, still wanting what he shouldn't have.

Tamra lay beside Mary, who snored a bit too loudly. Restless, she glanced at the clock and saw that it was almost one o'clock in the morning. She'd been staring at the ceiling for hours, trying not to toss and turn. But it wasn't the other woman's snoring that kept her awake.

It was Walker.

She'd given him her room, offering him a private place to sleep. But picturing him in her bed was making her skin warm. When she touched her lips, intent on reliving his kiss, she knew she was in trouble.

She couldn't fantasize about Walker, not here, not now, not like this. Guilty, she climbed out of bed, cautious not to wake Mary.

What she needed was a drink of water. A tall glass, full of ice. Something to douse her emotions, to cool her skin.

As she padded down the hall, the floorboards creaked beneath her feet. Once she reached the kitchen, she stalled. Walker stood at the counter, drinking a glass of water, doing exactly what she had come to do.

He hadn't noticed her yet. He faced the tiny window above the sink, gazing out at the night. His chest was bare and a pair of shorts rode low on his hips. His hair, those dark, sexy strands, fell across his forehead in sleepless disarray.

Suddenly he turned and caught sight of her. The glass in his hand nearly slipped. She could almost hear it crashing to the floor.

"I'm sorry," she said. "I didn't mean to startle you."

"It's okay. I was just—"

He roamed his gaze over her, and she became acutely aware of her short summer nightgown, of the soft cotton material.

"Just what?"

"Thirsty," he told her.

"Me, too."

"Then you can have this."

He handed her his water, and she put her mouth on the rim of the glass, sipping the liquid, wishing she were tasting him. The ice crackled, jarring the stillness.

He continued to watch her, taking in every inch of her body. He seemed to like what he saw, the slight cleavage between her breasts, the flare of her hips, the length of her bare legs.

She took another sip of his drink and noticed that his nipples were erect. She wanted to drop her gaze, but she didn't have the nerve to glance at his fly, to be that bold in the middle of the night.

"I couldn't sleep," he said. "Not in your bed."

Tamra returned his glass, giving him the rest of the water. In the process, her hand touched his. "Why not?" she asked, her heart picking up speed.

"Because I kept imagining your scent on everything. The sheets, the pillowcase."

Dizzy, she took a deep breath, dragging oxygen into her lungs. "I don't wear perfume."

"I know. I can tell. You wear lotion. Whenever we get really close, I can smell it on your skin."

"It's just a moisturizer." She knew that was a dumb thing to say, but she didn't know how else to respond. He was looking at her with lust in his eyes, with a hunger so deep, she wanted to crawl all over him.

Right here. In his mother's kitchen.

"It's soft," he said. "Airy. Like the plants and flowers in the greenhouse at my family's estate." He set his glass on the counter and moved forward.

She swallowed, got thirsty again, envisioned his mouth covering hers. She knew he was seducing her, but she didn't care. She liked the erotic expression on his face, the deep, husky tone of his voice.

He took another step toward her, his feet silent on the faded linoleum. "I haven't been with anyone in months."

A vein fluttered at her neck. She could feel it, skittering beneath her skin. "It's been longer than that for me."

"I'm good at controlling my urges," he told her.

She stood perfectly still. He was only inches away, so close they struggled to breathe the same air. "So am I. But I can't seem to do that with you."

"Me, neither." He cursed, just once, before he dragged her into his arms, before he kissed her so hard, her head spun.

When he pinned her against the counter, she nearly wept. His mouth plundered hers, over and over, giving her what she wanted, making the moment last.

Heat. Intensity. A tongue-to-tongue sensation.

She gripped his shoulders; he cupped her bottom and pulled her flush against his body. Then they broke apart and stared at each other.

"We can't do this," he said. "Not here."

She nodded, fighting the pressure between her legs, the desperation he'd incited. "Then where?"

"I don't know." He pulled his hand through his hair. "I can't think clearly."

Neither could she. All she wanted was him. Walker Ashton. A boy she'd heard about since she was a child. A man she barely knew.

"We could go for a drive," he suggested. "In my car."

The SUV he'd rented, she thought. A vehicle with

four-wheel-drive and big backseat. Suddenly she felt like a teenager, a moonstruck girl who should know better. "What if your mom wakes up?"

"We'll leave her a note."

"And say what? That we decided to cruise around the rez in the middle of the night? Or drive to Gordon for a piece of pie?"

He made a face. "Do you have a better idea?"

"At least let me get dressed. Grab something from my room. Mary knows I'd never go out like this."

That made him smile. Apparently, he'd been willing to climb behind the wheel just as he was—halfnaked and much too aroused. "My clothes are in your room, too. Will you get me a shirt? A pair of tennis shoes?"

She nodded, but as she turned away, he latched on to her arm. She thought he was going to kiss her again, but he didn't. He frowned instead.

"What's wrong?" she asked.

"I don't have any protection."

"I'm on the Pill."

He was still frowning. "I thought you haven't been with anyone for a while."

"I haven't. But I prefer to be prepared."

He searched her gaze. "Because of the father of your baby?"

She let out the breath she was holding. "Yes."

"I can't make any promises, Tamra. No happilyever-afters. But I wouldn't do what he did. I wouldn't hurt you like that."

"Thank you." She realized they were whispering,

speaking in hushed tones, talking about something far more intimate than sex.

And this time when she turned away to get their clothes, he didn't stop her.

Walker drove into the night, traveling on a dirt road, thinking this had to be the most strangely erotic moment of his life. Tamra sat beside him with a shopping bag on her lap. He hadn't asked her what was in it. For now he was trying to decide where to park. The reservation was dark, eerie, beautiful. The land went on forever, with trees swaying to the moonlight. In the distance a coyote howled.

"I don't know how far to go," he said.

She turned to look at him. She'd changed into a sundress that sported a row of tiny buttons down the front. On her feet, she wore cowboy boots. He'd never seen a more compelling woman. Her hair was the color of a raven's wing, sleek and shiny and begging to be touched.

"With me?" she asked.

He blinked, wondered what she meant. Then it dawned on him. She was responding to his statement. The SUV hit a slight bump in the road, and he grinned. He knew how far to go with her. "I was talking about how far I should keep driving, where would be a good place to park."

"Oh."

She ducked her head and he suspected she was blushing. He reached over to slide his fingers through her hair, just for a second, just to feel the silkiness against his skin. "I'm going to do everything imaginable to you."

"Oh," she said again, only sexier this time.

Damn if he didn't want to pull over right now, right in the middle of the road. "How about over there?" he gestured to a copse of cottonwoods.

Tamra glanced out the window. "The river is that way. There might be people camped by the water."

"Then we'll go in the other direction." He cut across the terrain, closer to the hills, to a backdrop that took his breath away. He'd never made love in an area so vast, so romantic.

He parked beneath a jagged stretch of moonlight, where stars danced in the sky. "What's in the bag, Tamra?"

She clutched it to her chest. "A blanket. Some extra clothes."

"Extra clothes?" He touched her hair again, toying with a strand that looped across her cheek. "What for?"

"In case the ones we're wearing get torn."

Walker's pulse jumped. Excited, intrigued, far too aroused, he moved closer. "Does that mean we can go crazy?"

She chewed her lip, a girlish habit he'd seen her do before. "You kept warning me that we were going to tear off each other clothes and I——" she paused, leaned toward him "——thought we better be prepared."

He wasn't sure if anything could prepare him for this moment—this middle-of-the-night, heaven-help-him lust. Anxious, he took her in his arms, his hands nearly quaking. She held on to him, too, gripping his shoulders.

And then they kissed, as deeply as they could, tongue to tongue, heart to beating heart.

A second later they went mad. He attacked her dress, sending every last button flying. She did the same thing to his shirt, ripping the denim with feminine force.

When she climbed onto his lap, he thought he might die. He breasts were exposed, only inches from his mouth. She was jammed between him and the steering wheel, but she didn't seem to mind. So much for the blanket, he thought. She'd dropped it, along with their extra clothes, onto the floorboard.

He licked her nipples, switching sides, blowing on each one, making them peak. She pulled his head closer, encouraging him to suckle.

Desperate, he lifted her dress to her thighs, running his hands along the waistband of her panties. She moaned and rubbed against his fly.

He closed his eyes, opened them, smiled at her.

She was watching everything he did, trying to see in the dark. He turned on the dome light, illuminating the vehicle with a soft glow. He didn't care if it drained the battery. He could stay here, just like this, for the rest of his life.

His body was rock hard, thick and solid and eager to penetrate hers. Only, they were still half-dressed, still torturing each other with foreplay.

She looked incredible, with her luscious curves and golden-brown skin. Her neck was long and slender, and her nipples were damp with saliva.

His saliva. His hunger. His insatiable need.

"I could eat you alive," he said.

"Then do it." She rocked forward in his lap, creating friction, giving him a slightly shy, slightly sirenlike smile. "And I'll do it to you, too."

Every ounce of blood rushed straight to his groin. He had no idea how she could be so subtle yet so obvious. Women, he thought, were fascinating creatures.

"This could be a dream." He nuzzled her neck, tongued the shell of her ear and inhaled the fragrance on her skin, the lotion that drove him to distraction. "A wet dream," he added, dragging her into the backseat.

Once again, he hiked up her dress, but this time, he removed her panties, clutching the piece of lace. He wondered if she'd chosen them for him or if she always wore such sexy little underthings.

When he kissed her there—right there—she bucked against his mouth. Wanting more, he pushed her legs open even farther, showing her how naughty he intended to get.

She practically melted against him, dissolving like spun sugar. Then she took off her dress and boots, tossing them aside, offering him every inch of her naked body.

A sacrifice, he thought. A gift.

Within minutes—heart pounding, soul-spinning minutes—Tamra kept her promise, shifting her body so she could pleasure him, too. So they could make love to each other at the same time.

She dislodged his shorts and took him in her

mouth, making his stomach muscles quiver, making his blood swim.

Yet somewhere deep down, he knew this was more than an affair. This was their emotions, a blend of sex and sin, of passion and warmth, of unbridled affection.

A pleasure so deep, he feared he might drown.

He kept tasting her, licking her while she did erotic things to him. And when she climaxed, when she convulsed against his tongue, he fought the urge to come, too.

Knowing he couldn't let her take him all the way, he stopped her before it happened. She sat up and gazed at him, still glassy-eyed from her climax.

Finally she smiled at him, and he realized why. His shorts were halfway down his legs, and he was still wearing his shirt, the fabric she'd torn to smithereens. He grinned and tackled her, pinning her to the seat.

She wrestled with his clothes, and they went crazy all over again. By the time he was completely naked, she dug her nails into his skin, clawing him like a dark-eyed cat, a feline in heat.

He thrust into her, full hilt. She wrapped her legs around him, and they gazed at each other, trapped in a candid moment, in being as close as possible.

She grabbed on to the plastic handhold above her head, bracing herself for a deep, driving rhythm, telling him, without words, what she wanted.

He didn't disappoint. He took her, hard and fast, rough and dangerous.

There was no other way to describe their coupling.

The crush of their mouths, the clank of teeth, the greedy, frantic, carnivorous sensation of pounding straight into her.

The woman stealing his senses.

She made his mind spin, his breath catch, his heart nearly beat its way out of his chest.

Together, they let themselves fall. She clung to him, gasping in his ear, shuddering in his arms. He came, too, spilling into her, warm and wet and drugging.

In the moments that followed, they remained still, afraid to move, to break the connection.

Finally he withdrew, leaving her damp with his seed. Unsure of what else to do, he grabbed his discarded shirt and tucked it between her legs, letting her use it like a towel.

"You're not sorry, are you?" she asked.

"No. Why would I be?"

"Because you said we were going to be sorry afterward."

"I said that before I knew you." He scooted next to her, smoothing her hair away from her face, thinking how beautiful she was.

"I'm not sorry, either."

He smiled, then noticed she looked chilled. He remembered the blanket she'd brought and climbed in the front seat to retrieve it.

"Here." He slipped it over her shoulders, and she invited him to share it with her.

He turned off the dome light, darkening the car, bathing them in the pitch of night. And as they snuggled in the dark, he wondered if they would be sorry later.

When he left the reservation without her.

Six

Morning came too soon. Tamra heard the clang of pots and pans, the familiar sound of Mary fixing breakfast.

Was Walker awake, too? Was he sitting at the kitchen table, pretending that he hadn't sneaked out of the house last night? Or crept back in several hours later?

She sat up and reached for her robe. She could still feel Walker's touch—his mouth, his hands, the strength of his body, the erotic sensation of flesh against flesh.

Although she kept telling herself it had been lust, a hard-hammering, desperate-for-sex release, she knew better. Because after the sex had ended, they'd remained in each other's arms, not wanting to let go, to break the spell.

And now, God help her, she was nervous about seeing him, anxious about facing the man who was seeping into her pores, the man playing guessing games with her emotions.

They were getting too close too fast, and it scared her. Yet she liked it, too. She envisioned marching into the kitchen or her bedroom or wherever he was and kissing him senseless. But she wouldn't dare, not in front of Mary. Walker's mom had slept through the entire event.

Tamra washed her face and brushed her teeth, but she didn't take a shower or get dressed. She simply tightened her robe and headed down the hall. She wanted Walker to see her this way, to look into her eyes on the morning after, to appreciate her tousled hair, to remember running his hands through it.

She entered the kitchen, but he wasn't at the table. She took a deep breath and decided he would awaken soon. He didn't seem like the type of man who would sleep the day away.

"Oh, my. Look at you." Mary turned away from the stove, from the old-fashioned oatmeal she was stirring. "Did you have a rough night?"

Tamra blinked, forced a smile, fought a wave of guilt. "Rough?"

"Did I keep you up?" The older woman sighed. "I was snoring, wasn't I? I need one of those mouth-piece devices. Or a nasal strip or something."

"It was fine. I hardly noticed." Because she'd been parked on the plains, having carnal relations with Mary's son.

A sin she was sure to repeat.

Dodging eye contact, she poured herself a cup of coffee, grateful it was thick and dark and blasted with caffeine. "Do you need help with breakfast?" she asked, adding sugar to her cup, giving herself another artificial boost.

"Sure. You can fry the eggs. But it's just the two of us. Walker already left this morning."

"Left?" Tamra spun around, nearly burned her hand on the sloshing drink, then set it on the counter. "He went home?"

"No, honey. He drove to Gordon. He said he had some banking matters to take care of."

Her pulse quit pounding. There were no banks on the rez, no financial institutions. "That makes sense."

Mary checked her watch, then went back to the oatmeal. An early riser, she was already dressed for work, wearing a freshly laundered uniform and squeaky nurse-type shoes. Her gray-streaked hair was tucked behind her ears. "Walker seemed preoccupied today."

"He did?" Tamra opened a carton of eggs, took inventory, tried to behave accordingly. "How so?"

"I think he was anxious to see you, hoping you were awake."

"Really?" A teenybopper reaction, a bevy of wings took flight in her belly, making breakfast an impossible task. But she cracked several eggs into a pan, anyway, then realized she'd neglected to turn on the flame. She glanced up and noticed Mary watching her. She'd forgotten the oil, too.

"What's going on with you two?"

"Me and Walker?" Caught red-handed, Tamra faked her response, feigning a casual air. "Nothing. We're just friends."

"Friends, my foot," his mother said. "I think you have your eyes on each other."

Uh-oh. Trying to stay calm, she dumped the mistake she'd made into a bowl, deciding she would fix scrambled instead of fried. And this time, she put a pad of butter in the pan, igniting the stove. "Would it be okay with you if we did?"

"Did what?"

"Had our eyes on each other."

"Of course it would," Mary told her. "But I'd hate to see you do something rash."

Unable to keep pretending, she gazed at the lady who'd raised her, who'd given her everything a child could hope for. "I already slept with him."

"Oh, my goodness." Mary fanned her face. "So soon?" She turned off the oatmeal, ignoring their half-made breakfast. "You need to be careful, honey. And so does he. This is all so new."

"We can handle it."

"Are you sure?"

"No," she admitted, "I'm not. But what choice do we have? We're already involved."

"For how long?"

"It doesn't have to last forever. And he promised he wouldn't hurt me."

The older woman frowned. "Not purposely, no. But what if you fall in love with him? What then?"

It was a question Tamra couldn't answer. A question she feared. Because she knew that when Walker went home, she would have to cope with her loss.

With missing him desperately.

Tamra tried to focus on her job. She sat at the desk in her cluttered office, telling herself to quit thinking about Walker. She had more important issues to deal with: flyers to design, schedules to coordinate, donations to secure for an end-of-the-month powwow.

Obsessing about a man wouldn't accomplish a thing.

A knock sounded on her door and she reached for her coffee, her second cup that day. "Come in," she called out, assuming it was Michele. Her friend had offered to stop by to help with the powwow details. The Oyate Project intended to host a raffle this year, giving away as many prizes as they could wangle.

She glanced up, saw that she was mistaken. It wasn't Michele. Walker crossed the threshold, wearing jeans and a denim shirt, similar to the one she'd torn off his body.

He moved closer, and her heart went haywire.

"Hi," he said.

"Hi." She started stacking folders, trying to compose her senses, trying to look busy, to pretend that she hadn't been thinking about him. "I wasn't expecting you."

He reached for an ancient folding chair in the corner and opened it, positioning it across from her. A pair of mirrored sunglasses shielded his eyes, and his sleeves were rolled to his elbows.

"Do you have a minute?" he asked.

For him, she had all day. All night. All year. "Sure. What's going on?"

"I just got back from the bank."

"Mary told me that's where you went."

"I opened a checking account in Gordon. I figured that would be the most convenient location." He removed his sunglasses and hooked them onto his pocket. "You and Mary will have to go into the branch to fill out some paperwork. Unless you already do your banking there. Then I can add your names online."

She merely blinked at him. "I don't understand."

"What's not to understand? It'll be a joint account. I'll make a deposit every month, and you and Mary can use it for whatever you need."

"You're volunteering to support us?"

"Not completely, not unless you want to quit your jobs. But I don't see that happening. You're both so dedicated to what you do."

"Then why are you doing this?" She sucked in a much-needed breath, wondering how he could sit there—-so damn casually—and offer her money. "Is it because you slept with me?"

A sudden flare of anger burst into his eyes, like fire. Like brimstone. Like a man who was used to controlling other people's lives. "What the hell is that supposed to mean? That I'm trying to turn you into my mistress?"

"That's how it seems," she said, refusing to be intimidated by his temper, the all-consuming power that could drain a woman dry. The muscle ticking in his jaw. The hard, ready-to-explode, king-of-the-universe breathing.

He stood and pushed away his chair, nearly shoving it against the file cabinet. "I was just trying to help. To make life easier for my mom." He paused, drilled his gaze into hers. "And for you, too. But I don't keep mistresses. I don't reward my lovers for sleeping with me."

She didn't say anything, so he leaned forward, bracing his hands on her desk. "I can't believe you think so little of me. Don't you get it, Tamra? Don't you see why this matters to me?"

"No, I don't. Mary and I can take care of ourselves."

"I know. But my mom's car looks like it's on its last leg and you're lending money to friends, cash you can barely spare. I don't want to go home and worry about you."

She sighed, wishing she hadn't provoked an argument. Walker was confused, she thought. And he was comparing his life to hers. "You don't have to feel guilty for being rich."

"Easy for you to say, Miss Do-Gooder."

She rolled her eyes, trying to ease the tension, to make him stop scowling. It was the best she could do. Other than fall prey to his machismo and touch him. Kiss him. Tug his stubborn mouth to hers. "Listen to you, Mr. Write-a-Check."

He smiled in spite of himself. Grateful, she flicked

a paper clip at him. He grabbed the worse-for-wear chair and parked his butt down again.

"You should see my office at Ashton-Lattimer," he said. "And my condo. Not to mention the apartment I have on my family's estate in Napa Valley. It's inside the mansion, on the second floor with a spectacular view."

She couldn't even fathom his lifestyle. Edward had been wealthy, but not compared to the Ashtons. "Those are the kinds of things Mary wanted you to have."

"Will you talk to her about the account?" he pressed.

"No, but you can. If you want to help your mom and she's willing to accept your offer, then it's okay with me. But I don't want to be part of it."

"Because you're not comfortable taking money from me?"

"Edward used to give me gifts. He used to buy me trinkets."

"That jerk who hurt you? It's not the same thing."

"When it ended, when he broke up with me, I felt cheap." And for her, it had been the worst feeling in the world. "I don't want to go through that again. Not ever."

"Don't compare me to him. We're nothing alike."

She almost reached across the desk to hold his hand, but she curled her fingers, keeping her distance, recalling the ache that came with being in love. She couldn't bear to fall for Walker, not like that.

"Will you at least accept a check for your charity?" he asked.

She looked into his eyes and saw the sincerity in

them. And then she realized how foolish she was, refusing to hold his hand, to touch him. She knew they were going to sleep together again. Sex was inevitable. "You already wrote one, didn't you?"

"Yep." He removed it from his pocket and handed it to her.

She glanced at the denomination. "That's a generous donation." And sex wasn't love, she told herself. There was nothing wrong with continuing their affair.

"It's tax deductible." He picked up the paper clip she'd tossed at him. Toying with the metal, he altered the shape, bending it back and forth. "Besides, it's for a worthy cause. I know the Oyate Project will put it to good use."

"Thank you." She wrote him a receipt, and when she gave it to him, their eyes met and held.

An intimate look. A deep, heart-thundering stare.

"Will you come home with me, Tamra?"

"Home?"

"To Napa Valley. To the estate."

Panic, instant anxiety, leaped to her throat. His family's mansion? The winery? The place where he grew up? She shifted her gaze, breaking eye contact, dragging air into her lungs. "What for?"

"Because I want to take you and Mary there. It would be the perfect place for my mom to meet Charlotte. And you and I could spend some time together."

"What about the rest of your family? Spencer's wife? Your cousins?" When she and Mary lived in Northern California, they used to scan the society pages for tidbits about the Ashtons, and they'd come across their names quite a few times. "They might not like us staying there."

"Spencer is dead, and he's the only one who would have forbidden it. The others won't interfere."

"That's not the same as welcoming us."

"Fine. Whatever. If I tell them to welcome you, then they will."

His bulldozing did little to ease her mind. "I'm not sure if I can get the time off."

"I'm only asking for a week. Seven measly days. You don't take vacations?"

"Yes, but—"

"But what?"

Tamra fidgeted with the paper clip he'd bent. What could she say? That she was nervous about being thrust into his world? That she didn't belong there?

"I'm sure Mary would be more comfortable if you came with us," he said. "And so would I."

"Would this include a trip to San Francisco?" she asked.

"Definitely. It's only fifty miles from the estate. And it's where I live most of the time, where I work."

"How often do you commute to Napa Valley?"

"On the weekends mostly. But I've been spending more time at the estate since Spencer was killed. I can't help but miss him."

She glanced out the window, felt the cloud of death that floated between them. "I'd like to visit Jade." To kneel at her baby's grave site, to whisper to her little girl.

"We can visit her together. We can take her the flowers I promised." He released a rough breath. "We can do other things, too. Just the two of us. But we'll have to tell my mom what's going on. We can't keep sneaking around."

"I already told her."

"That we're lovers?" He sat back in his chair, frowned a little, pulled his hand through his hair. "How'd she take it?"

"She said we needed to be careful. That this is all so new."

"But it won't be." His gaze sought hers, holding her captive. "Not after we get to know each other better."

"Then I'll go with you. I'll arrange to take some time off." To be with him, to meet his high-society family, to discover who Walker Ashton really was.

Walker sat on the steps of his mother's porch. Tamra was still at work, and Mary was inside, puttering around the kitchen, doing whatever domestic things women did. She'd returned from her job about an hour ago, giving him the opportunity to talk to her, much in the way he'd spoken with Tamra earlier. And just like her non-Hunka daughter, she'd left him with mixed emotions.

Good and bad, he supposed.

"You're not brooding, are you?"

"What? No." He turned to look at Mary, who'd come outside with a glass of lemonade in her hand.

She handed him the drink. "Then you must be deep in thought."

"Maybe. I don't know." He took a sip and noticed that she'd added just the right amount of sugar.

"Are you upset about the checking account?"

"That both you and Tamra turned me down? Yeah, it bugs me. I'm trying to do the right thing, and no one will let me."

She sat beside him. "The thirty thousand Spencer gave me was enough. I don't want to take money from my own son, too."

He squinted at her, trying to shield his eyes from the late-day sun. "I thought Indian families were supposed to help each other. I thought that was the message around here."

"It is. But I'm not poor anymore. I'm not struggling to pay my bills." She smoothed her blouse, a polyester top she'd probably bought at a discount store. "I was ashamed of my house when you first got here, but it was wrong for me to feel that way. It's nicer than what most people have around here."

In Walker's eyes she was still poor. Not destitute, like the out-of-work population on the rez, but a two-bedroom mobile home and a tired old Buick certainly didn't make her rich. "At least you and Tamra agreed to go to California with me. I'm glad about that."

"So am I. I can't wait to see Charlotte."

"She's anxious to see you, too." A rabbit darted by, scurrying into the brush. He watched it disappear, feeling like a kid who'd missed out on his childhood, a boy who'd grown up too fast. "I wish you'd reconsider about the money."

"Goodness gracious. You're just like your father."

"Stubborn?" he asked.

"Pigheaded," she replied.

He snorted like a swine and made her laugh. He knew they were still trying to get used to each other, to have stress-free conversations. "Did my dad have a temper, too?"

"Not as bad as yours."

"Gee, thanks." He bumped her shoulder, and she smiled. He wondered if his father was watching them, if angels existed. Walker couldn't remember his dad, at least not to any degree. But he couldn't remember his mom, either, and she was sitting right next to him.

She sighed, her voice turning soft. "I loved David so much."

Suddenly he didn't know what to say. He'd never been in love. He'd never given his heart to anyone. A bit lost, he stared at the grass, at the coarse, wild groundcover.

"Do you know how I met him?" she asked.

"No. How?"

"I was hitchhiking, and he picked me up. It was my second day on the road, and I wasn't getting very many rides."

"Is that the first time you left the rez?"

She nodded. "I was twenty-three years old, determined to get away from this place and never come back."

"Where were you headed?"

"Omaha. I figured it was big enough to find a job and start my life over."

"Did my dad offer to drive you there?"

"No. He offered to take me as far as Kendall, the town where he lived." Her tone turned wistful. "You should have seen me when I climbed into his truck. Talk about nervous. He was so handsome, so tall and strong, with the greenest eyes imaginable."

Curious, Walker studied her, noticed how girlish she seemed——a woman reminiscing about the man she loved. "I guess you never made it to Omaha, considering Charlotte and I were born in Kendall."

"David offered me a job. He said he was looking for a housekeeper, someone to cook and clean for him and his farmhands. But later I discovered that he just wanted to keep me around."

Walker couldn't help but smile. His old man must have been quite the charmer. "Crafty guy."

"And proud and kind. Everything I could have hoped for. I don't think I'll ever stop missing him."

He glanced away, then frowned, his memories as tangled as the weeds spreading across the plains. "What happened on the day he died?"

"Your father had a heart attack behind the wheel. I was with him, riding in the passenger seat. We were on our way home from the mortgage company, trying to get them to discount the loan, but it was too late. They refused to work with us, to help us save the farm."

"Did you try to take the wheel?"

"Yes, but I couldn't. Everything happened so fast. We hit a tree. Between the heart attack and the accident, David didn't stand a chance."

"Charlotte and I were at a neighbor's house. An elderly woman." He remembered a gray-haired lady, but he couldn't recall his own parents.

Mary blinked back tears. "She was a widow who used to baby-sit now and then. That's where you stayed until Spencer came and got you."

"What did my uncle tell her?"

"That he was going to care for my children until I was well enough to take you to the reservation. She had no reason to question his motives."

As silence stretched between them, he placed his lemonade on the step. The glass had been sweating in his hand, making his palms damp. He wanted to comfort Mary, to abolish her pain, as well as his own. But he didn't know how. He was still struggling to bond with her, to behave like her long-lost son.

"I should get started on dinner." She stood and dusted off of her pants, looking old and tired.

He got to his feet, envisioning her when she was young, like the pictures he'd seen in her photo albums. "How do you say mother in Lakota?"

"*Iná,*" she told him.

"*Iná,*" he repeated.

Her breath hitched, causing a lump to form in his throat. "I'll help you with dinner," he said, even though he was a lousy cook.

She touched his cheek, her hand warm against his skin. They gazed at each other, but they didn't embrace. Before things got too awkward, she led him into the kitchen, where she taught him how to make Indian tacos.

Walker was out of his element, but he did the best he could, trying to please his mother. By the time Tamra arrived on the scene, he was knee-deep in fried dough, lettuce, tomatoes and a pan of ground beef.

Tamra pitched in, and the three of them prepared the evening meal. But soon, he thought, they would be in Napa Valley. On the estate. The mansion where he was raised.

The place Walker called home.

Seven

The weather in Northern California was perfect, a warm summer day bursting with color. The wine country, with its fertile land and prospering grapes, was surrounded by mountain ranges that rose to the sky.

Tamra sat next to Walker in his car, a silver Jaguar he'd retrieved from a long-term parking lot at the airport. Mary settled in the backseat, but she'd been relatively quiet since they'd arrived in Napa Valley.

Walker stopped at a gate at the entrance of the estate, pressing a keypad with a security code. As they continued, moving closer to their final destination, Tamra drew a shaky breath.

The mansion itself, an enormous cream-colored structure accented with marble, presided from a hill overlooking the vineyards below. A large circular drive boasted an elegant reflecting pool. The water shimmered in the sun, catching the light like magic.

"Oh, my," Mary said, a statement that seemed to convey exactly what Tamra was thinking.

Oh, my.

"The humble abode," Walker joked, pulling into the driveway with ease.

He was glad to be home, Tamra thought. To the familiarity of his youth. But his comfort zone only made her more nervous.

To her, the estate seemed like a rich-and-powerful fortress. It had Spencer Ashton written all over it. The dead man still reigned.

"Long live the king," she mumbled.

Walker shot her a quick glance. "What?"

"It looks like a castle," she amended.

He shrugged and killed the engine of his sixty-thousand-dollar car. They climbed out of the Jag, and he gestured to the trunk, where he'd already popped open the lid. "Don't worry about our luggage. Someone will take care of it soon enough."

Someone? The hired help? "You're spoiled," Tamra said.

He frowned at her. "I don't have servants in San Francisco. I prefer my privacy. But things are different here."

She held her tongue, and he opened the door to an expansive foyer. A magnificent library was on the left and a lavish dining room on the right. A double staircase, leading to each wing of the house, made a sweeping impression. Walker escorted her and Mary into a majestic room he called the grand parlor.

Grand indeed: creamy fabrics and ornate antiques, a terrace that presented a breathtaking view of a flourishing garden and the vineyards below.

Tamra didn't want to sit, although Walker offered her and his mother a seat. The furniture, she noticed, was polished to perfection. Tables gleamed and mirrors reflected every carefully decorated angle. There wasn't a thread out of place. Even the tassels on pillows displayed themselves in a don't-touch-us manner.

A woman wearing a black uniform draped with a white apron entered the parlor. She looked about Mary's age, her long dark-brown hair pinned up.

"Mr. Walker," she said, her tone soft and respectful. "It's good to have you home. And with your new family."

"Irena." He greeted her in a detached voice. But even so, he introduced her to Tamra and Mary, letting them know she was the head housekeeper.

If his attitude hurt Irena's feelings, she didn't let it show. Her blue eyes sparkled, especially when she spoke to Mary. Tamra liked her immediately, which made Walker's disposition even more baffling.

Had the housekeeper done something to displease him? Or did he treat all of the employees with mild disdain?

Tamra shifted in her seat. Was it a learned response he'd picked up from Spencer?

"Miss Charlotte and Mr. Alexandre left a message for you," Irena informed him. "Their flight was delayed. They won't be arriving until tomorrow morning."

He frowned. "That's fine. Is Lilah here?"

"Yes, Mr. Walker. She'll be with you shortly."

"Thank you. Will you send in some refreshments?"

"Yes, of course. I'd be glad to." She excused herself and gave Walker's mother a gentle smile on her way out the door.

Mary seemed disappointed about Charlotte's delay, but Irena's kindness had prompted her to relax, helping Tamra relax, too.

Five minutes later, when Lilah Spencer breezed into the parlor, their discomfort returned.

The lady of the manor, a reed-thin redhead, approached Walker with a Hollywood-style kiss, brushing her lips past his cheek. Impeccably dressed, she donned a cream-colored suit that matched the decor. Her makeup was flawless, her skin unnaturally taut.

Botox injections? Tamra wondered.

"I see the Indian people are here," Lilah said.

"Mind your manners," Walker told her, scolding his forty-nine-year-old aunt as if she was a child.

"Was that politically incorrect?" She divided her gaze between Tamra and Mary. "Would you prefer Native American?"

So much for the welcome Walker had promised, Tamra thought. "Indian is fine."

"Well, then. See?" Lilah smoothed her lapel, where a simple gold broach had the audacity to shine, to look as chic as the woman wearing it. "No harm done."

Walker introduced his mother first, and Mary was

gracious enough to extend her hand. Lilah extended hers, too, and Tamra wondered if Spencer's widow was mimicking what she saw, like a Stepford wife who kept switching gears, not quite sure how to treat Mary—the Indian her dead husband had wronged.

Irena arrived with a silver tray bearing iced tea, fresh mint, lemon wedges and sugar. Another maid carried a platter of finger sandwiches and a delicate assortment of fine china.

Lilah made a face at the tea, as though she craved something stronger. The head housekeeper offered the first glass to Mary, who accepted it gratefully. After the drinks were distributed and the sandwiches left in a buffet-style setting, the hired help disappeared.

"Now, then." Lilah sat in a Victorian settee and crossed her legs, her posture as graceful as an aging fashion model. "We need to decide what rooms Mary and Tamra should occupy."

Walker made the decision in two seconds flat. "My mother can take Charlotte's old room, and Tamra can stay in my apartment."

"Your apartment?" Lilah arched her lightly penciled bows.

"That's right," he countered, daring her to challenge him.

She didn't. She backed down easily, but not without a socially acceptable response. "His apartment is in the west wing," she announced to no one in particular. "And it has two bedrooms."

Walker gazed at Tamra from the across the room, and her heart bumped her chest. Fat chance that she would be sleeping in the second bedroom. She and Walker hadn't made love since that night on the plains. They'd decided to wait rather than take liberties at Mary's house. Of course, Walker was going full throttle now, demanding Tamra's attention.

"Will you and your guests be joining us for dinner?" Lilah asked her nephew.

"Yes, we will."

"Then I'll see to the menu." She stood, tall and slim and regal. "If you're weary from your flight, don't hesitate to retire to your room," she said to Mary. "I understand how taxing jet lag can be." She turned to Tamra. "You, too." Then to Walker, "I trust you'll show them to their quarters."

"Absolutely."

"I'll make sure the luggage is taken right up," Lilah concluded. She bade everyone a courtly farewell and left the parlor to tend to her duties.

A queen who was lost without her king.

Walker's apartment was as exceptional as the rest of the mansion, although the decor was quite a bit bolder, with more use of color. It contained a stylish living room, two bedrooms, two bathrooms and a comfortably equipped kitchen. The paintings on the walls exhibited desire, rage, even sadness. They were, Tamra thought, a reflection of Walker's personality.

Their luggage had arrived in no time, and she decided to unpack while Walker sat on the edge of his bed and watched her.

"Is there an another apartment on the other side of us?" she asked.

He nodded. "It belongs to my cousin Trace. He got the balcony."

She looked up, shook her head. "God forbid he should get something you don't have."

Walker rolled his eyes. "Trace irks me."

She reached for a hanger. "Really? How so?"

"He just does. We've always been at odds with each other."

Masculine rivalry? she wondered. Or did it go deeper than that? "Have you ever tried to work things out with him? Talk about your differences?"

He barked out a cynical laugh. "Yeah, right. He's impossible to communicate with."

"What does he do?"

"He manages the Ashton Estate Winery."

"How come you didn't get into that business?"

"Because Spencer wanted me to work with him at Ashton-Lattimer Corporation. The investment banking firm." He removed his shoes and socks and tossed them on the floor. Today he wore a charcoal suit that darkened the color of his eyes.

"Trace is Spencer's son, right?"

"Yep. His only son with Lilah."

"How many daughters do they have?"

"Two. Paige and Megan. Paige still lives here, and Meagan is married now." He took off his jacket. "Can we quit yapping about my family and get cozy?" He roamed his gaze over her, lowered his voice. "I've missed you."

Tamra's skin turned warm, but she refused to give in so easily. "You've missed touching me. That's not the same as missing someone. And I'm not through asking questions."

He made a goofy expression, then pretended to hang himself with his tie. She bit her lip to keep from laughing. "That's not going to charm me into bed," she told him, even though she wanted to tackle him, to kiss him, to let his sexual frustration consume her.

"Then hurry up and finish this interview. I've got a woman to seduce."

"Fair enough." She hung her best dress, black cotton with satin trim, in his closet. "What's the deal with Irena?"

"She's the head housekeeper. I already told you that."

"Why were you so rude to her?"

"I wasn't rude."

"The hell you weren't."

"Okay. Fine. Irena is a traitor. She's been with us since I was a kid and she let her daughter—who also used to work here, I might add—get engaged to the enemy."

"The enemy?" The Ashton Estate was beginning to sound like the setting for a soap opera. Days of Our Disgruntled Lives. "Who on earth are you talking about?"

"Eli Ashton. The SOB who threw a fit about Spencer's will and the Ashton-Lattimer stocks I inherited."

Money, she thought. The root of all evil. Only in

this case, she didn't know if Eli was the evil party or if Walker fit the bill. "How is Eli related to your uncle?"

"He's one of Spencer's kids with Caroline Lattimer, a former wife. The other Ashton family." He walked over to a mini bar in the corner and poured himself a shot of tequila, the first time Tamra had seen him drink. "They have a boutique winery about twenty-five miles from here. But that's not enough for Eli. He'll probably try to steal the Ashton-Lattimer stocks away from me."

"Did Spencer leave Caroline's children anything in the will?"

"Nope."

"And you don't think that's wrong?"

"It's not my place to judge my uncle's decision. Besides, Eli is only making a fuss because his grandfather on his mother's side founded the investment banking business."

"But Spencer ended up with it?"

"Caroline's father left it to him. Of course that was before Spencer divorced her. Then again, it doesn't really matter because their marriage was never legal. Spencer had a wife in Nebraska a long time ago, but he never divorced her."

Tamra could only stare. Her head was twirling like a top. "And what was her name?"

"Sally. He has grown kids with her, too. Oh, and there's a little boy Spencer fathered two years ago."

"He cheated on Lilah?"

"As far as I know, he cheated on all of his wives.

Lilah was one of his mistresses before he married her. She was his secretary. The old make-out-in-the-office routine."

"And this is the man you admired?"

Walker gave her a disturbed stare. "He treated me better than he treated everyone else. What am supposed to do? Hate him for that?"

"No, but you shouldn't be rude to Irena because her daughter is engaged to Eli."

"We're back to that?"

"That's right, we are. Did you really expect Irena to stop her daughter from falling in love?" She paused, looked at him, felt her heart pick up speed. "Love isn't something a person can control. Not a parent, not a child, not a man or a woman."

He frowned, squinted, left his empty shot glass on the bar. "What if Eli contests the will?"

"Then he contests it. That doesn't have anything to do with Irena. You owe her an apology, Walker."

"Listen to you. The voice of compassion." He sat on the edge of the bed again. "But you're right, I do. I'll apologize to her tonight, sometime before dinner. After all, she can't help it if her daughter fell for a selfish jerk."

Tamra doubted that Eli was the moneygrubber Walker was making him out to be. She suspected there was more to the story, and Irena had supported her daughter's decision for all the right reasons. "Good parents try to make their children happy."

"You're talking about Irena, right?"

She gave him a solemn nod. She certainly wasn't referring to Spencer.

Walker gazed out a second-story window, and she followed his line of sight. She couldn't see the view from her perspective, but she suspected he was gazing at his family's vineyards, the way he'd studied Mary's land allotment while he'd been on the rez.

Was he comparing the Napa Valley wine country to the South Dakota plains?

"My mom wants me to be happy," he said.

"Yes, she does. Mary loves you very much."

"I know. I can feel her affection." He turned away from the window. "But I don't understand it. She barely knows me."

Tamra walked away from the closet, taking a seat next to him on the bed. "Most mothers have a special bond with their children. I never knew my baby at all. But I loved her." She placed her hand on his knee, recalling the day she'd buried Jade. "She'll always be in my heart."

He touched her face, running his knuckles along her jaw. A masculine caress, a man-to-woman need. "I wish it was that easy for me. That I could love Mary the way she loves me."

"You will. Someday you will."

She put her head on his shoulder, and he held her so tight she could hardly breathe. But she didn't care. She wanted to be as close to him as possible.

He released the top button of her blouse, and she

lifted her head, grateful, so incredibly grateful, for his seduction.

As he kissed her neck, as his lips sought her skin, she opened her shirt completely, allowing him access to her bra, to the cleavage between her breasts.

He accepted the offering, putting his mouth all over her, leaving warm, damp marks. Branding her, she thought, taking possession.

They slid onto the bed, lying side by side, caressing, kissing, making each and every sensation count.

Sweet and slow. Dark and sensual.

He removed her bra, then skimmed his hand down her stomach, popping the snap on her jeans, playing with the waistband of her panties. When he moved lower, she caught her breath.

They rolled over the bed, scattering pillows, rumpling the quilt. Wanting more, they took turns undressing each other. And by the time she got to his trousers, he was hard and thick and desperate to straddle her. But she worked his zipper slowly, teasing him, making him wait.

"That's not fair," he said.

"Isn't it?" Tamra found her way into his boxers and skimmed the tip of his arousal, where moisture beaded like an iridescent pearl. She rubbed it onto his skin, and his entire body quaked.

"Not fair at all," he reiterated.

"You're impatient," she whispered in his ear.

"Can't help it." He kissed her, swirling his tongue, making love to her mouth.

She finished undressing him, and his breathing accelerated. Finally, when they were flesh to flesh, he braced himself above her.

But he didn't push her legs apart. He simply gazed at her, taking in every feminine curve. Then he cuffed her wrists with his hands, holding her arms above her head, making her his prisoner.

Tamra could only imagine how she looked, her nipples peaked, her areolae several shades darker than her brown skin.

"You're the most compatible lover I've ever had," he said.

"Have there been a lot?"

"It depends—" he lowered his head and flicked his tongue over one of her breasts "—on what someone considers a lot."

She didn't try to free herself, even though he still held her captive. She liked his game, his decisive maneuvers.

Sexual strategy. Her heart pounded with anticipation.

A strand of hair fell across his eyebrows, making him seem like a rebel. She itched to run her fingers down his spine, to sink her nails into his back.

But he offered her something even better. In the blink of an eye, he rolled over and took her with him, shifting until she was poised above him, with her legs sprawled across his lap.

"Want to go for a ride?" he asked.

Her breath rushed out; her pulse stumbled. She envisioned riding him until the end of time, until the sun disappeared and the moon spun in the sky. "Yes."

"Then do it." He gripped her waist. "Do it to both of us."

She didn't have a choice. She wanted him so badly, her life could have depended on it. More than ready, Tamra lifted her hips and slid down, taking him inside.

His fingers tightened around her waist, moving her up and down, setting the rhythm.

Deep, wet, intoxicating.

She leaned over to kiss him, to suck on his tongue. Desperate sex, she thought. Suddenly Walker tasted like the tequila he'd drunk.

Or was that the flavor of passion? Of the heat between them? The spiraling sensation of liquid fire?

They made love like animals on the verge of an attack. He lunged forward, so they were face-to-face, so she could look directly in his eyes while they practically tore each other apart.

She clawed his chest, raking her nails over every muscle. He ravaged her shoulders, using his teeth, nearly bruising her.

"This is insane," she said.

Beautifully crazy.

He didn't respond. He just encouraged her to keep going, to keep milking his body with hers.

Harder, faster, deeper.

The room twirled in a haze of color. Daylight burned bright. She could almost feel the sun melting over her skin, dripping in sweet, sticky rivulets.

A hot, hip-grinding climax shattered inside her, making her shudder, making the wetness between her legs seem like honey.

And then she realized that Walker had spilled into her, that the dampness had come from him.

Her lover.

The man sweeping her away.

Eight

Tamra stepped out of the bathroom with a thick, fluffy towel wrapped around her. Everything at the Ashton Estate was luxurious.

Too luxurious, she thought, as she walked over to Walker's dresser to get some fresh undergarments.

He lounged on the bed with a towel wrapped around him, too. After they'd made love, they'd taken a shower together, but she'd remained in the bathroom to apply her makeup and blow-dry her hair.

His hair, she noticed, was still a little damp, combed away from his face and styled with a dollop of gel.

He smiled at her, and she slipped on her bra and panties and put her towel in a nearby hamper. Once she found the courage to return his smile, she looked through her side of the closet. She didn't want him to know how nervous she was about having dinner with his family.

"Do the Ashtons dress for their meals?" she asked.

"Nope." He drew his knees up, nearly flashing her. "We eat naked."

She sighed, almost laughed, wished he wasn't so damn charming. "You know what I mean."

"Lilah always dresses for dinner, but you don't have to worry about that. Just wear whatever feels right."

She scanned her modest selection and decided on a white skirt, a white blouse and a beaded belt she'd bought from a Lakota craftswoman. She added a noticeable array of silver and turquoise jewelry she'd acquired over the years.

"Now you really look Indian," Walker said.

She turned to face him, preparing for a fight. "Is that a problem for you?"

"No. I like it."

She let out the breath she was holding. "Thank you."

"You're welcome." He frowned a little. "I'm not ashamed of your heritage, Tamra. Of my heritage," he added. "I'm comfortable with who we are."

"Are you?" she asked, hating how temporary their affair was, how throwaway it suddenly seemed.

A fire ignited in his eyes. "What's that supposed to mean?"

"You would never relocate to Pine Ridge."

"Is there a reason I'm supposed to?"

Caught in an argument of her own making, she fussed with a wide silver bracelet, tightening it around her wrist, squeezing the edges of the metal. "No, of course not."

He didn't drop the subject. "It's a bit late for me to start my life over, to move in with my mom and pretend that we haven't been separated for twenty-two years. Besides, how would I survive on the rez? I'm the interim CEO of an investment-banking firm."

"Interim? You took over Ashton-Lattimer when Spencer died?"

"I was the executive vice president before he was killed. I'm the logical choice."

"So you think the board is going to vote you in permanently?"

He nodded. "I'm on a leave of absence right now. But as soon as you and Mary return to Pine Ridge, I'm going back to work. I imagine it will happen then."

She gave her bracelet another tight squeeze. "And you're going to accept the position?"

"Of course I am. Why wouldn't I?"

She shrugged off his question, as well as the intensity in his eyes. She had no right to challenge his choices. He'd already warned her that happily-ever-after wasn't in the cards.

Then why did she feel so dejected? So fearful of losing him?

"I'm going to check on your mom," she said.

"Dinner isn't for another hour."

"I know, but I want to see how she's settling in."

Tamra put on her shoes and ventured down the

hall, leaving Walker alone in his apartment. She didn't worry about getting lost since Mary's room was located in the west wing, near the upper foyer. She knocked on the door and received an instant welcome.

The older woman smiled, admiring Tamra's ensemble. "You look pretty."

"Thank you." She noticed Mary was dressed in her ratty bathrobe, with hot curlers in her hair, looking as nervous as Tamra felt. "What are you going to wear?"

"I don't know. This place is so doggone fancy." Walker's mother pursed her lips. "What do you think of my wake dress?"

"I didn't know you brought it."

"I figured I should."

"In case someone died?"

"Goodness, no." Mary looked at her, and they both laughed. "In case I needed a simple black dress."

"I think it's perfect."

Mary breathed a sigh of relief, and Tamra helped her get ready, hoping the Ashton dinner didn't feel like a wake.

An hour later they were seated in the formal dining room. The table was graced with fresh-cut flowers, elegant china and pristine linens.

Walker and Trace, the cousin he'd complained about, had acknowledged each other brusquely, but Trace had greeted Tamra and Mary in a much-warmer tone. Tamra thought he was handsome with his athletic build and stunning green eyes. She also sensed that his passions ran deep, that there was more to him than Walker was willing to admit.

Paige, the other cousin who lived at the estate, seemed like a peacemaker, quiet and unassuming yet keenly aware of her surroundings. Her almond-shaped eyes darted between the two men. Was she hoping they would quit giving each other the cold shoulder? Come to their senses and behave like family?

Lilah, on the other hand, pretended not to notice. She dined on the first course, a silver fork in her hand and a row of pearls looped around her neck.

Tamra wished someone would say something. That a conversation would flow. She glanced at Paige, who gave her a comforting smile. Blond highlights dazzled her light-brown hair, framing her face in soft layers. She was, Tamra thought, a breath of fresh air in an otherwise tense situation.

Lilah finally broke the silence. "Do you like your room?" she asked Mary.

"Oh, yes. It's lovely," Walker's mother responded.

"It's been redecorated since Charlotte was a child." Lilah took a bite of her watercress salad, chewed, swallowed, then continued speaking. "I had no idea that you were alive. Spencer told everyone, including me, that you'd died with your husband."

Mary looked at her son, then returned her gaze to Lilah. "I appreciate you taking care of my children."

"Well, yes, of course." The redhead almost fumbled with her fork, proving that she hadn't been happy about Spencer bringing home two half-breed kids. "Charlotte was so shy. I never knew what she was thinking. Now Walker—" she paused to nod her head at him "—he's a bit more predictable."

"Stubborn?" Mary asked.

"Precisely." Lilah sighed. "At least with me. He behaved wonderfully for Spencer."

"Hey." The man in question shifted in his seat, then winked at Mary, teasing her with his "stubborn" charm. "That's not fair. You two can't gang up on me."

His mother smiled at him. "I think we just did."

When Lilah agreed, everyone at the table relaxed. A moment later Irena entered the dining room, informing Lilah that there was an important phone call for her.

Lilah thanked the head housekeeper and excused herself. But when she returned after a short absence, she gripped the back of her chair.

"It was Stephen Cassidy," she announced.

Walker looked up. "Spencer's attorney? Is there news about the will?"

She shook her head. "Stephen heard some rumors about the murder investigation."

Spencer's murder, Tamra thought, as Lilah's knuckles turned white.

"The police are building a case against Grant." She all but spat the suspect's name. "They're going to put that traitor behind bars."

"Are you sure?" This came from Paige, who blew out an anxious breath. Trace was on edge, as well, waiting to hear what else his mother had to say.

She continued in a tight voice. "Supposedly the authorities uncovered something that could be highly damaging, something that goes beyond circumstantial evidence."

"What is it?" Trace asked. "What did they find out?"

"Stephen wasn't able to secure the details." Lilah resumed her seat and reached for her wine, downing the contents much too quickly. "I just wish this nightmare would end. That I could stop envisioning my husband with a bullet in his heart."

"Who's Grant?" Tamra asked.

"Spencer's son by his first wife," Walker responded.

"The one in Nebraska?"

"Yes, but she's been gone a long time. She died when Grant and his twin sister were about twelve." Walker picked up his knife and stabbed his roll. "Grant doesn't have an alibi for the night Spencer was shot, and he was at my uncle's office earlier that day, arguing with Spencer. If what Stephen heard is true, then it's only a matter of time before the police arrest him." He cut the roll into several jagged pieces. "I hope that bastard goes to hell for what he did to my uncle."

Tamra studied the darkness in her lover's eyes, the pain of losing his mentor.

Dinner had, indeed, turned into a wake.

Even if no one eulogized Spencer, he was there.

The murder victim. The man someone, possibly Grant Ashton, hated enough to kill.

As the morning sun shone in the sky, Walker sat beneath a veranda located behind the house. Lost in thought, he scanned the gardens, the plants and flowers that flourished in the dew-misted air.

Tamra sat next to him at a glass-topped table. Charlotte, Alexandre and Mary were there, too. Walker had watched his mother and his sister embrace. He'd seen Charlotte cry in Mary's arms.

Even Alexandre had hugged Mary with ease. And he'd called her *Maman,* French for *Mother.* It had flowed from his lips naturally, and he was only the prospective son-in-law.

Walker had never seen Mary so happy. She and Charlotte paged through the photo albums Mary had brought, the family pictures that had yet to jar Walker's memories.

Why couldn't he remember his parents?

"Look how handsome Daddy was," Charlotte said. She leaned toward Mary, studying David's image.

"And look how beautiful you are." Mary touched her daughter's cheek, clearly awed by the young woman she'd become.

Walker had to admit that his sister was beautiful, with her long streaming hair and petite yet willowy figure. She wore a flowing summer dress, as bright as the garden that surrounded them.

"Charlotte runs Ashton Estate Botanicals," Walker said, gesturing in the distance. "The greenhouse is that way." More flowers, he thought. More plants.

"I plan to set up an independent nursery," his sister added. "But for now, I'll remain at Ashton Botanicals, training someone to take over for me."

"An independent nursery?" Mary asked. "Away from the estate?"

Charlotte nodded. "I haven't decided if I'll establish it in Napa Valley or in France. But either way, it will be my own company."

"That's wonderful. Your father had a green thumb. He could make anything grow."

Yes, Walker thought, their dad had been a farmer. A man who'd lived off the land. Sometimes he wondered why he himself hadn't been born to Spencer and Lilah instead of David and Mary.

A moment later the thought shamed him, making him feel like the worst kind of bastard. He moved his chair closer to the table. "May I have that?" He motioned to a photograph of David, Mary, Charlotte and him. The last picture of all of them together, taken on New Year's Day in 1983. The year their lives had changed forever.

Mary glanced up and snared his gaze. "Of course you can." She removed the faded snapshot and handed it to him.

"Thank you." He pressed it to his chest, just a smidgen away from his heart. "I won't lose it. I'm going to scan it into my computer so I can make a copy."

His mother smiled. "I trust you."

Charlotte and Alexandre smiled at him, too. Self-conscious, Walker cleared his throat. Tamra put her hand on his knee, and he turned to look at her, wishing he could kiss her, hold her, let her absorb his tangled emotions.

"Oh, Mama," Charlotte said, breaking the silence. "It's so wonderful to have you here. To be with you.

When I was a little girl, I would dream of you. Imagine a day like today." She paused, and her voice hitched. "Somewhere deep down, I never believed that you were dead."

Alexandre touched his fiancée's shoulder. *"Ma petite,"* he whispered, lending his support.

The women turned teary-eyed, and Walker wished he could love as deeply as his sister, that he could be more like her. But he wasn't a dreamer. He'd never questioned the tale Spencer had told him. He'd trusted his uncle.

"Will you give me a tour of the greenhouse?" Mary asked her daughter.

"Yes. And you must stay with Alexandre and me, at our new home." Charlotte turned to Walker. "Would that be all right with you?"

"Sure," he said, knowing he couldn't interfere with the precious time his mom and his sister had. "Tamra and I will go to San Francisco while Mom stays with you. Then we can all get together before they go back to Pine Ridge."

"That sounds perfect." Charlotte reached for Mary's hand. "Alexandre and I are going to visit your home, too. As soon as we can arrange a trip."

"Maybe you can come for the powwow at the end of the month," the older woman said.

"A Sioux gathering?" Charlotte beamed. "I've always wanted to be close to my heritage. To know more about it."

"Then I'll teach you." Mary squeezed her hand. "Your father always told me that I should be proud of my culture. That I should encourage you and your brother to be proud. But I kept losing sight of that."

"Is that why he wanted me to have a shield?" Walker asked.

His mother nodded. "A shield reflects a warrior's medicine, everything in his life. Protection in combat, success in the hunt, being a good lover, finding the right mate. Even visions and dreams are represented."

He wished he had visions and dreams. Something beyond Ashton-Lattimer. "That's a nice sentiment."

"It's more than sentiment. It projects who you are." Mary scooted closer to him. "I can make you a shield, the way I'd originally intended to. Or I can teach you how to make one. You can put your own symbols on it. Animals, colors, anything you want."

Would a shield bind him to the Oglala Lakota Sioux Nation? Or would it be a forgery? He'd told Tamra that he was comfortable with his heritage, but was that a lie? Would he stop being Lakota when he returned to Ashton-Lattimer? When he started behaving like a corporate *wasicu* again? Or a brash, citified *iyeska?*

"Walker?" his mother pressed.

"What?"

"Do you want me to make it? Or would like to create it yourself?"

"You can do it." He glanced at the picture of his family. "But will you put something on it that represents us?" He lifted the photograph. "You, Dad, Charlotte and me?" He released a ragged breath. "And Tamra, too?"

Tamra looked up at him, and he wondered if he should have kept quiet instead of mentioning her name. Although she smiled, she seemed surprised, maybe even a little shy, about what he'd said.

Mary glanced at his lover, then back at him. "She's good for you. You're good for each other."

"I think so, too," Charlotte said.

"Oui," Alexandre offered his opinion, as well. "I agree."

Okay, great. Now that everyone had just embarrassed the hell out of him, Walker didn't know how to respond. His relationship with Tamra wasn't meant to last. He wanted her to be represented on his shield because he was going to lose her.

And lose a piece of himself after she was gone.

Several hours later Walker sat at the oak desk in his extra bedroom. He scanned the picture on his computer, created a "family photos" file and printed it. Next he saved it on a disc and packed it for the San Francisco trip.

He was used to switching computers. He had a PC at both home locations, as well as a laptop he carried for airports, hotel rooms and places in between.

Tamra knocked on the open door, and he turned to look at her.

"I noticed some ice cream in your freezer," she said. "Is it okay if I dig into it?"

"Sure." He roamed his gaze over her and saw that she'd changed into a pair of sweats, preparing to relax in his apartment. "Will you get me a bowl, too?"

"Okay. I'll be right back."

He watched her leave, then put the original picture in an envelope and left it on his desk with a self-sticking note, reminding himself to return it to his mother.

Tamra came back, balancing two glass bowls. She'd scooped a mound of Neapolitan into each, with spoons readily available. She handed him one of the frozen treats and sat on the edge of the bed. He remained in the swivel chair.

She started eating the vanilla ice cream first, and he wondered if it was her favorite flavor. He continued to analyze every bite she took. Finally she finished the vanilla and started in on the strawberry. He changed his mind, deciding she liked chocolate the best since she was saving it for last.

Walker had mixed all three flavors up in his bowl, stirring the concoction like pudding.

"Your sister is amazing," she said. "Sweet, bright, beautiful. I really like her."

"She appeared to like you, too."

"Alexandre is amazing, as well."

"Really? You think so?"

"Oh, yes. He's gorgeous. So—" she stalled when Walker raised his eyebrows at her "—attentive to Charlotte."

Envy nipped at his heels, but he let it go. He knew Alexandre was one of those guys women noticed. All those fancy French words. Even his mom had swooned a little. "He loves my sister."

"I can tell." She toyed with her spoon. "It was

weird...what Mary, Charlotte and Alexandre said about us."

"Yeah, weird." He shifted his gaze. "They think we're good for each other."

When silence pulled like taffy between them, he stirred his dessert again. He hated these magnified moments. He wasn't good at easing the tension.

But she got past it quick enough.

"Does anyone ever stay in this room?" she asked.

"No. I never invite guests here."

"Then why do you have an extra bed?"

"I don't know. To fill up space, I guess."

She took her first bite of the chocolate ice cream. "What about your bedroom?"

He nearly cursed beneath his breath. Silence had been safer than the conversation she'd hatched. "No one stays there, either."

"I am," she said.

"Yes, but you're—" he paused, afraid he would say something too revealing "—different."

"Different?" she parroted.

Crafty girl, he thought. Prodding him to spill his guts. "I already told you that you're the most compatible lover I've ever had. I wanted to take advantage of that."

She sucked on her spoon, and he wondered if she was trying to seduce him. If she was, her ploy was working. He couldn't keep his eyes off her mouth.

He dropped his gaze and noticed her nipples through her T-shirt. "Are you cold, Tamra?"

She almost smiled. "I'm eating ice cream."

"Want to christen the bed?"

She gave him an innocent look, then shook her head and laughed. "You're easy, Walker."

So she had been playing a game.

He left the desk, came closer, took away her bowl and nudged her down. "You drive me crazy." He unzipped his jeans and slipped her hand inside. "More than crazy."

She closed her fingers around him, and they kissed, deep and wet and slow. She tasted like chocolate, and the flavor, the sweetness, aroused him even more.

They dragged off each other's clothes, tossing articles onto the floor, leaving cotton and denim in their wake.

She lowered her head, then used her mouth between his legs. He tugged his hands through her hair and felt his blood soar. Oh, yeah, he thought. She drove him crazy.

She paused, looked up at him and made his world spin.

Mind-blowing foreplay. Sexual surrender. He wanted it all. And he wanted it with her.

He lifted her up and kissed her, tongue to tongue, flesh to flesh. He needed to get her out of his system, to drink her in, to drain her of every last drop.

Desperate, he guzzled her like the wine he'd been reared on, getting drunk, forcing the intoxication through his veins.

But he wanted to make her drunk, too, so he went down on her, giving her the oral pleasure she'd given him.

She arched, rubbed against him and fisted the quilt.

He kept doing it, teasing her, urging her to completion.

When she stopped shuddering, he rose above her. And with one powerful thrust, he entered her. She gasped, and he went deeper, submerging himself in wetness, in warmth, in everything he craved.

Sunlight spilled into the room, making summer hues dance across the bed. They clasped hands, their fingers locking.

A bond. A connection. A feral need.

Walker wasn't about to let go.

And neither was she. She wrapped her legs around him, holding him hostage, keeping him unbearably close.

Every cell in his body screamed for a release, but he wanted to make it last. To keep making love to her. Yet he couldn't.

Heaven help him. He couldn't.

Her lotion rose like a mist, filling his nostrils. The scent of seduction. Of heat, he thought. Of a life-altering orgasm.

He looked into her eyes, then let himself fall.

Hard and fast.

As hard and fast as a man could endure.

Nine

Walker's condominium in San Francisco was in the same upscale district as Edward's. Yet Tamra hadn't realized it before now. But why would she? She'd only seen Walker's driver's license once, on the first day they'd met, and she hadn't paid attention to his address, to the zip code that would have revealed the location.

"What's wrong?" he asked, as they stood on his deck, overlooking a view of the city.

"Nothing. Your home is beautiful."

"Come on, Tamra. I can tell something is bothering you. You're acting strange."

She took a deep breath, then shifted to look at him. They'd arrived about ten minutes ago and he'd given her the grand tour: spacious rooms, ultramodern furniture, a hot tub. Luxurious, bachelor-style living, she thought. "Edward lives about six blocks from here."

"Jade's father? The sperm donor?" Walker frowned, his dark eyes turning even darker. "Are you going to be thinking about him the whole time you're here with me?"

"Of course not. It's just a coincidence. It doesn't mean anything."

"The hell it doesn't." He turned away and scowled at the city. "Edward still upsets you. He still matters."

"Losing my baby still matters. And this was a shock, that's all. I hadn't expected you to live near him." She moved closer, trying to shed her anxiety, to control the situation, to lighten her lover's mood. "His place isn't as nice as yours. It's not as high up. His view sucks."

Walker managed a smile. "Are you trying to stroke my ego?"

"Did it work?"

"A little, yeah." His smile turned a bit too sexy. "But stroking something else would work even better."

She smacked his shoulder, and they both laughed. She suspected they would be tearing off each other's clothes before the sun went down. A second later she glanced at the gazebo-framed hot tub. "I've never done it in one of those."

"Really?"

"No. Have you?"

"Yes, but I'm not giving you any details. No kiss and tell."

"That's fine." She didn't want to envision other women at his condo, to create their faces, to hear their names. For now she wanted to pretend that Walker Ashton belonged to her. That he would always be her exclusive lover. Hers and hers alone.

When he gazed into her eyes, her heart jumped, playing leapfrog in her chest.

"Maybe Edward doesn't even live around here anymore," Walker said.

"It's only been three years," she responded, her voice quavering.

"A lot can happen in that amount of time." He continued to look in her eyes. "We've only known each other for a few weeks."

Sixteen days, she thought, but who's counting?

He touched her cheek and her knees went weak. In an ordinary world, they would be little more than strangers. But their world was far from ordinary. They'd become lovers almost instantly. And now she was pretending that he belonged to her, that it was okay to make up stories, to fool her mind.

"Do you miss this city?" he asked. "Do you miss it at all?"

She shook her head, recalling the flavor of the place she'd left behind: cable cars, China Town and the Golden Gate Bridge, the roller-coaster landscape and Victorian houses, the early-morning fog.

Too many memories, she thought. The place where Jade rested in a tiny grave.

"Do you miss the reservation?" she asked him.

"I wasn't there long enough." He lowered his hand, skimming the ends of her hair, letting it slip through his fingers.

Already she could feel herself losing him.

Tamra nearly panicked, nearly gasped for the air that refused to fill her lungs. Was she falling in love? Only deeper this time?

Walker wasn't Edward. He wasn't the father of her lost child. But she wished he was. She wished they'd made a baby together.

He watched her, much too closely. "You're upset again."

"I don't mean to be."

"But you are."

"Just hold me." She reached for him, and he put his arms around her.

Eyes closed, she nuzzled his neck. He brought her closer, and she inhaled his scent, the aftershave that lingered on his skin.

Had she fallen in love? After only sixteen days? Was she losing her mind? "I can't think clearly."

"Why not?"

"I don't know." She clung to him yet she knew she should let go. "Maybe it's your fault."

"Don't blame me. You wanted to come to San Francisco."

"To visit Jade." Not to lose her heart. Not to let Walker strip the layers of her soul.

He rocked her in his arms. "Then we'll visit her."

"Not right now," she heard herself say. She needed

time to compose herself, to change the direction of her thoughts. "Let's do something else."

"You could come to the office with me."

She blinked, stepped back. "You're going to work?"

"I'd like to check in, let my assistant know that I'll be in town for a few days. Besides, I want you to see Ashton-Lattimer."

"Then that's where we'll go." And maybe, she thought, just maybe, the corporate environment would bring her back to reality.

And keep her from dwelling on love.

Thirty minutes later, Tamra and Walker arrived in the Financial District. Ashton-Lattimer Corporation was located in an eighteen-story structure on California Street.

Once they were inside, Tamra looked around the lobby and noticed the turn-of-the-century architecture. Walker had told her that the building had been constructed in 1906, after the great fire. He seemed fascinated by the history connected to it.

She tried to keep her emotions in check, but on the elevator ride to the top floor, the walls started closing in. They were the only two people in the confined space. He'd changed into a suit and tie, looking like what he was: a tough, charming CEO. Spencer Ashton's favored nephew. She could almost see the older man's blood flowing through his veins.

Like poison, she thought.

He smiled at her, and a lump caught in her throat. She knew Walker had a tender side. The side he must have hidden from his uncle.

"You okay?" he asked.

She cleared the raspy sound from her voice. "This is an imposing place."

"I suppose it is. Maybe more so since Spencer died here. He was shot in his office. He was working late and—"

The elevator doors opened and he stopped speaking, letting his words fade into the walls. She wondered if he would ever stop mourning his uncle. If he would accept Spencer for the bastard he was.

The fourteenth floor, where the Ashton-Lattimer executives made their corporate marks on the world, presented a modern decor.

Walker introduced her to a few of the secondary bigwigs, men who treated him with the utmost respect. She wondered if there were any women at the top of the food chain.

Finally he showed her his office—a spacious state-of-the-art domain in shades of gray, with silver-framed watercolors, a shiny black desk and floor-to-ceiling windows. Walker was a man rooted to the city.

This wasn't déjà vu. This wasn't Edward all over again. Being with Walker in San Francisco created a whole new stream of emotions.

New fears. New challenges.

Letting Edward go had been her salvation, a part of her growth, of who she was destined to become. But losing Walker—

"Come on," he said, cutting through her thoughts like a machete. "I'll introduce you to my assistant."

He escorted her to a smaller office, but apparently

the woman at the lacquered desk wasn't who he expected to see. "Kerry?" He gave her a curious study. "Where's Linda?"

Kerry came to her feet, and Tamra did her damnedest not to stare. Tall and curvaceous, the stunning blonde wore a lavender suit and chic yet understated jewelry. Her eyes, a color that could only be described as violet, were framed with dark, luxurious lashes.

Talk about beautiful. This girl had it all.

Tamra prayed she wasn't a former bed mate of Walker's. An office liaison. A hot-tub bunny. She couldn't deal with feminine rivalry, not now, not today.

"Linda called in sick," Kerry said. "She caught that awful flu that's been going around, so I'm covering for her."

"Fine. No problem. You're more than qualified." Walker sent the Ashton-Lattimer employee a professional smile, then turned to Tamra and made the introduction.

Kerry, whose last name was Roarke, extended her hand with genuine warmth, and Tamra knew, right then and there, that she'd never slept with Walker. There was nothing between him and the breathtaking blonde, not even a passing interest.

"Kerry used to be Spencer's executive administrative assistant," he said. "After he died, she transferred to Human Resources, but she helps out wherever she's needed."

Now Tamra wondered if Kerry had been involved with Spencer. Given his penchant for infidelity, she could only imagine how badly he'd probably wanted her.

But was Kerry the type to sleep with a married man?

While Walker and the blonde talked business, Tamra sat in a leather chair. Every so often, she stole a glance at the other woman, still wondering about her.

Finally the meeting ended.

After Walker took Tamra's hand and led her out of the building, he stopped to kiss her, to brush his mouth across hers.

As a moderate breeze swirled around them, she decided that she was ready to visit Jade's grave, to bring her daughter and the man she loved together. Because after Tamra was gone, Walker would remain in San Francisco, keeping Jade from being alone.

Tamra gave Walker directions to the cemetery, but he stopped at a florist first. She wandered around the flower shop, her thoughts spinning like a pinwheel.

She didn't want to go home without telling him that she loved him. Yet she wasn't sure if a confession was in order. What did she hope to accomplish by admitting the truth? Did she think it would change the status of their relationship? That he would abandon his corporate lifestyle and move to Pine Ridge with her?

Fat chance, she thought. Love wasn't a miracle.

But what was the point of keeping quiet? Of suffering in silence? She studied a bouquet of daisies, feeling like a schoolgirl who couldn't temper her emotion-laced whims.

He loves me. He loves me not.

Walker was Mary's son. He would always be part of Tamra's life. Seeing him from year to year was inevitable. She couldn't ignore the connection they shared.

"What about pink roses?" he asked, his voice sounding behind her.

She turned, looked into his eyes. Mary had warned her in the beginning about getting hurt, about falling in love. But now Walker's mother thought he and Tamra were good together.

"Pink roses?" she parroted.

He nodded. "With baby's breath. And maybe a toy, too. Something fluffy. They have teddy bears. A lamb that's really cute. The florist said they can add a toy to the arrangement."

She wanted to put her arms around him, to hold him close. He seemed like Jade's earthbound angel. Her tall, dark, masculine protector. "That sounds perfect."

"Okay." He smiled. "I'll be right back with the stuffed animals. We'll have to choose which one we want."

Tamra glanced at the daisies again.

He loves me. He loves me not.

Walker returned with a pink teddy bear in one hand and a white lamb in the other. He held them up, wiggling each toy, making them come to life. "Which one do you like better?"

"I don't know." The teddy bear had big expressive eyes and the lamb offered a tender smile. "Why don't you decide?"

He made a puzzled face, giving the stuffed animals a serious examination. "Maybe we should get both. The other one might feel bad if we leave it behind."

Tamra wondered how this could be the same man who'd allowed Spencer Ashton to influence him, to guide him, to mold and shape him into the adult he'd become.

She couldn't imagine Spencer buying toys for a baby's grave. Or, heaven forbid, worrying about the emotional welfare of a white lamb or a pink bear.

"Thank you, Walker. This means a lot to me."

His gaze locked on hers. The cozy flower shop, with its festive colors, refrigerated cases and vine-draped displays, made him look even more masculine. Bigger, broader, stronger in the sun-dappled light.

"Jade is going to be happy to see you. To know you're here," he said. Then he paused for a moment, mulling something over in his mind. "When we get back to Napa Valley, we should take my mom to my dad's resting place."

Tamra couldn't quit looking at him. A strand of hair, loosened from the San Francisco breeze, cut across his forehead, slicing over one dark eyebrow. She had the notion to smooth it into place. Just to touch him, she thought. Just to tempt her fingers.

"Charlotte will probably do that," she finally said.

"You're right. She probably will." He cradled the stuffed animals. "I'll go put in our order. Let the saleslady know what we want."

While they waited for the floral arrangement, she inhaled the gardenlike fragrance, the softness in the air. Walker stood with his hands in his pockets, his designer suit and silk tie still in place.

Tamra wore the same clothes she'd had on earlier. She hadn't changed to go to his office, but she hadn't needed to. Her denim dress and tan cowboy boots reflected her style, who she was and who she would always be.

They arrived at the cemetery, silence fluttering between them. He carried the roses, and she led him through grassy slopes, where ancient trees burst with summer foliage. The headstones scattered across the lawn varied, some fancy, others simple. The one that belonged to Jade was white, with an eagle feather etched upon it.

Tamra knelt, dusting away leaves that had fallen.

"Jade Marie Winter Hawk. Beloved daughter." Walker read the baby's marker, then placed the basket on the ground. Nestled among the flowers, the bear and the lamb faced each other, smiling like friends on a preschool playground.

"Marie was my mother's name." She envisioned Jade the way she might look today—a three-year-old with mixed-blood features, a sweet, beautiful, half-Lakota child.

"It's a pretty name. All of it."

"Thank you." Memories clung to her mind like cobwebs, but she didn't want to cry, to let her daughter know she was sad.

"Will you tell me what happened?" Walker asked.

She nodded, then took a deep breath. "Most fetal deaths occur before labor begins, and that's what happened to me. I suspected something was wrong because she'd stopped moving."

"I remember you mentioning that before. I can only imagine how scared you must have been."

"Afraid and alone. Except for Mary. Your mom was there to comfort me." She dusted another leaf from Jade's grave, where the wind had stirred it from a nearby tree. "An ultrasound confirmed my suspicion, and that's when the doctor broke the news to me."

He reached for her hand, slipping his fingers through hers. Grateful for his touch, she continued her story, wanting to share her past with him. "There was no medical reason for immediate delivery, so they gave me the option of inducing labor or waiting for it to happen on its own."

"Did you induce?"

"Yes. Most women in that situation do. It's too traumatic to wait." She searched his gaze and noticed how closely he watched her, how much he seemed to care. "After I delivered, the hospital did an extensive evaluation, an autopsy and some other tests. They discovered that Jade died from a birth defect. But it wasn't caused by something that's likely to recur in another pregnancy. The risk that I'll deliver another stillborn baby is low."

He brought their joined hands to his lips and brushed a kiss across her knuckles. "You'll have more children someday."

"Yes, someday." Tamra decided she was going to tell Walker that she loved him. Tonight…tomorrow morning…she wasn't sure when. But one way or another she was going to summon the courage to say those three little words out loud.

Just so he knew how she felt. Just to hear his response. Just to see the reaction in his eyes.

Ten

At dusk Walker and Tamra sat on his deck, sharing takeout Chinese food. A mild breeze blew, awakening the aroma of kung pao chicken, sweet-and-sour pork, egg rolls and fried rice.

They used paper plates and plastic utensils, something Walker did often. He rarely fussed in the kitchen, cooking or dirtying dishes.

"I was wrong," Tamra said.

"About what?" He stabbed a piece of the kung pao chicken, a spicy Szechuan dish with just enough kick to ignite his taste buds.

"I thought we'd be tearing off each other's clothes before the sun went down."

He glanced up at the sky and saw a small stream

of light drifting through the clouds. "There's still time." He watched the golden light shift and fade, then sent her a teasing grin. "But we'll have to hurry."

She managed an appreciative laugh, and he was glad to hear the uplifting sound. He'd been worried about her all day, hoping her anxiety would lessen.

He knew that Edward's proximity, the home her ex-lover owned in the area, had triggered her emotions. This town held a lot of sadness for her. A lot of grief. But Walker wanted to change that. He wanted to give her some warm and caring memories.

He figured that a casual dinner was a good start. His redwood deck offered a romantic ambience, with outdoor lanterns and citronella candles. A wind chime near the back door created a melodious tune, and the hot tub was ready and waiting, steam rising from the water. Plants flowered all around it, vines twisting and twining on the gazebo lattice. He liked the jungle effect, as well as the privacy it afforded him.

Tamra ate another small helping of the sweet-and-sour pork, and he watched her add extra chunks of pineapple to her plate. They occupied a rustic wood table that complemented her unpretentious beauty, her blue-jean dress, the slightly scuffed boots she favored.

He shifted his gaze to the hot tub, thinking about the conversation they'd had earlier. "That isn't the spa I made love in."

She looked up from her food. "It isn't?"

"No. It happened somewhere else."

"Thank goodness." She reached for her bottled

water. "Now I don't have to envision you and another woman splashing around in there."

Her envy, or whatever it was, pleased him.

He smiled and stole the biggest piece of pineapple from her plate, stuffing it into his mouth before she could stop him. "My spa is safe."

She shook her head, but he knew she was enjoying his company, the lazy evening he'd created.

Should he admit where the hot tub rendezvous happened? Break his kiss-and-tell policy? Give her details about his past? The infrequent wildness? The few-and-far-between times he'd sown his rich-boy oats?

Oh, what the hell, he thought. "It was at a college party. A drink-until-you-drop sort of thing."

Tamra made a face. "You did it at a party? With other people around?"

Walker frowned, realizing he should have kept his mouth shut. She probably thought he'd participated in an orgy. "It wasn't like that. The party was over. I was in the hot tub with a blonde who lived there. And my friend, Matt, was in one of the bedrooms with her roommate."

She made another face. "Did you switch partners?"

"I wouldn't have done that." He paused, pondering Matt's sexually abundant lifestyle. "Of course, my friend might have."

"He sounds like a great guy."

Walker ignored the sarcasm in her voice. "He is. Honestly. He's a good person. He's just not the kind of guy I'd let any of the women in my family date." He glanced at the fortune cookies they'd yet to break open. "Don't ask me why he ever tried his hand at marriage. I knew he'd end up divorced."

"Is he wealthy? Does he come from an Ashton-type environment?"

"He's rich. But he earned every cent himself. Matt Camberlane didn't have a damn thing when he was growing up. He was probably as badly off as some of the people in Pine Ridge."

She tilted her head. "And you befriended him?"

He shrugged off her surprise. "I was poor once, too, remember? Before Spencer took Charlotte and me in. I understood Matt's shame. As well as his determination to succeed." He scooped up a forkful of rice. "We're still friends."

"Then I'll try not to judge him." Her gaze slammed into his. "But I agree. You should keep him away from the women in your family."

"I'm not worried about it. I'm sure Matt has enough lovers to keep him entertained."

"And you have me."

The air in his lungs whooshed out. The impact of her words, the depth at which they affected him, belied the *entertainment* aspect of their conversation.

"You're not my toy, Tamra. It isn't like that between us."

"I know." She pushed away her plate. "God, how I know."

He noticed her hands were trembling, that she was riddled with anxiety again. He didn't know what to do, how to respond. He feared their relationship was spinning out of control, like a runaway train, a derailment that would leave them bruised. Battered. Wounded.

"There's something I need to tell you." She fidgeted with a bracelet around her wrist. "I wasn't sure when would be the appropriate time, but—"

She stalled, and he scooted his chair back, scraping the wooden deck. He'd been sitting too close to the table, too close to her. Because somewhere in the seed of his soul, in the cavern of his mind, he knew what she was going to say.

"I love you, Walker."

The words came, just as he'd expected. And so did the panic that erupted inside him. "No one has ever been in love with me," he managed. "No one."

"I am."

She searched his gaze, piercing him with her admission, with raw, agonizing honesty. He knew he shouldn't be scared. He was a single, unattached male who had nothing to lose.

Nothing but his heart.

Did he love her, too? Was all the craziness love? The desperate need? The way he longed to protect her? His fear of losing her? Of surviving without her by his side?

Walker picked up his water and took a long, hard swallow. But the ice-cold liquid didn't sober him. He should've figured it out before now. He should've known. "It's happening to me, too. You're not alone in this."

"Oh, God. Really?" She closed the food cartons, keeping herself busy, nearly dropping the leftover egg rolls. Nervous. Excited. "What are we going to do?"

"I don't know." His pulse zigzagged, beating frantically beneath his skin. "Can't we just ignore it? Forget that we talked about?" He sent her an anxious smile. "Maybe just go nuts in the hot tub instead?"

She smiled, too. But it was just as shaky, just as unsteady as his. "Trust a man to look for sex as the answer."

"You can't blame a guy for trying." He couldn't think of anything else to do, so he stood up and gathered the cartons she'd closed. "I'll put these away."

She rose to her feet, as well. "I'll wipe down the table and throw away the trash."

Cleanup duty took a matter of minutes, which left them in the kitchen, staring at each other beneath bright, blinding lights. He wondered if they should have taken the fortunes out of their cookies, used those silly little slips of paper for encouragement.

"We'll figure something out," he said.

"We will?"

"Sure." He ventured closer to her. One, two, three steps and he was close enough to smell the lotion on her skin, the scent that never failed to linger in his mind. "People fall in love all the time."

"People who live over a thousand miles away from each other?"

"So we've got an obstacle to overcome." He smoothed a strand of her hair. "I'm good at solving problems."

She touched his hair, too, running her fingers through it. Within seconds they were locked in each other's arms, kissing and caressing.

And then she took his hand and led him outside. Together they stepped into the shelter of the gazebo, into the maze of plants and low-hanging vines.

Without speaking, without words to clutter their thoughts, they undressed, dropping their clothes onto the deck. He brought her naked body next to his, letting the sensation arouse him even more.

And as they slipped into the water, he decided there was nothing to worry about.

All he had to do was ask her stay, to leave the reservation and move in with him. It was, he decided, the only answer. The only logical choice. And he would talk to her about it. But not yet, he thought.

Not just yet.

Hands questing, they touched. Everywhere. Skin to skin. Water swirled around their bodies, making steam rise to the surface. He could see her through the haze, as dark and exotic as the night. The sun had set, making way for the moon, for a soft, silvery glow.

He lifted her up, placing her on the edge of the tub. She looked like a siren, he thought, an indigenous goddess from the sea, with her legs spread just for him.

He took her hand and encouraged her to touch herself.

Shy. Erotic. Daring.

The woman he was falling in love with.

He tasted her, licking and kissing between her fingers. She watched him, rubbing and purring, making sweet, naughty sounds.

Walker feared he might explode.

She climaxed, and he dragged her into his arms, desperate to fulfill his fantasy.

To claim Tamra Winter Hawk as his own.

Tamra's head was reeling. From the aftermath of sex, she thought, from the hot, bubbling water and cool San Francisco air. But most of all because Walker Ashton admitted he was falling in love with her, too.

He wrapped her in a towel, and she looked up at him through the chlorine-scented moisture dotting her eyelashes.

Her pulse wouldn't quit pounding.

He grabbed another towel and dried himself off with haste, then secured the terry cloth around his waist. "Let's go inside. I have a robe you can borrow."

She followed him into the condo. She liked the idea of wearing something that belonged to him, of letting it envelop her in warmth.

She waited in the living room, and he returned with a navy blue robe that was thick and plush and far too big.

"It's perfect," she said.

For himself, he'd thrown on a pair of jeans. But his chest was still bare, and water dripped from his hair in jewellike rivulets. Already Tamra itched to touch him again.

"Will you have a glass of wine with me?" he asked.

"Are you trying to get me drunk?"

"So I can take advantage of you? You bet." He gave her a devastating wink. "The lady found me out."

Her heart ricocheted, bouncing off the walls of her

chest. "Okay. But just a little. I'm not much of a drinker."

"No problem." He poured a small amount for her and gave himself a generous helping.

She tasted the Pinot Noir, but since she wasn't a connoisseur, she didn't comment on the flavor. "Is this from your family's winery?" she asked instead.

"Absolutely." He turned the bottle, where he'd placed it on an end table, so she could examine the label. "Nothing but the best."

They sat quietly for a while, and she snuggled deeper into the atmosphere.

"I want you to move in with me, Tamra."

Suddenly a strong, cold dose of reality ripped through her veins. "Here?"

"Yes, here. This is where I live. And I want to share my life with you."

Everything inside her went still. He was asking her to be with him, to stay him, yet how could she say yes? How could she live in the city? Pretend to be someone she wasn't?

Tamra clutched his robe. His scent was on it, she realized. The faded fragrance of wood smoke, of male spice.

She closed her eyes, opened them, felt her body go numb. Was she making a mistake? Would she regret this decision for the rest of her life? Would she cry for him on those long, lonely South Dakota nights?

"I can't leave Pine Ridge," she said, the words nearly sticking in her throat. "I'm meant to be there. To try to make a difference. To help our people."

"This isn't about our people." With her rejection blazing in his eyes, he downed his wine, swigging it like beer, his manners falling by the wayside. "This is about us. You and me."

"Why can't you move?" she asked, the glass in her hand vibrating. "Why can't you relocate?"

"Me? Living on the rez? That would never work, and you know it. My background is in investment banking. That's what I do. That's what's in my blood. How am I supposed to walk away from that? I don't belong in Pine Ridge."

"And I don't belong here."

"You have a degree in marketing," he argued. "You'd do well in San Francisco. You'd fit right in. You've lived here before."

She shook her head, tears flooding her eyes. She couldn't leave the land of her ancestors, the place she'd struggled to accept, to become part of. "Pine Ridge is my home."

His voice turned hard. "Then why did you tell me that you loved me?"

"Because I wanted you to know how I felt."

"For all the good it did." He refilled his wine, drinking it just as quickly, just as brutally as before.

She set her glass on the end table, next to the bottle. She would never use alcohol to pacify her pain. She'd seen too many people on the rez fall into that trap. "Slow down, Walker. That won't help."

"Don't tell me what to do." He stood up, looking tall and dark and edgy. "The last thing I need is the woman I love treating me like a child."

She drew her knees to her chest. They loved each other, yet they couldn't stay together.

He crammed his hands in his pockets, shoving his jeans down a little, making them fall lower on his hips. "All I've been thinking about is how awful it was going to be to lose you. But I'm losing you, anyway."

"Me, too. But I didn't expect a miracle," she said, recalling the warning she'd given herself earlier. "Deep down I knew you'd never change your lifestyle for me. That you'd never move to Pine Ridge."

"And you won't move here. So what damn difference does it make?"

He picked up the Pinot Noir again and frowned at the Ashton label, and for a moment she feared that he would throw the bottle, smash it against the wall. To just to hear it shatter, she thought. Just to release the tension she'd caused. But he held his temper.

And when their eyes met, when he looked straight at her, she knew she would never be the same. No matter how many years passed, no matter how hard she tried to erase him from her mind, he would always be the man she loved.

Walker and Tamra returned to Napa Valley a day early with discomfort humming between them. He'd dropped her at his apartment at the estate, claiming he had some local business to tend to.

From there he drove to his sister's house to talk to his mother. And now here he was, sitting next to Mary on a teakwood bench on Charlotte's flagstone patio. In the garden setting, trees, flowers and potted plants flourished, with rolling hills in the distance.

A fountain in the center of the yard drew his attention, making him frown. It looked like a wishing well, but Walker knew better.

He'd explained the entire situation to his mom, but she hadn't offered to help. She hadn't offered to do a damn thing.

"I want you to convince Tamra to move to San Francisco with me," he said, still frowning at the fountain. A family of finches was bathing in it, splashing and chirping, looking far too happy.

"Oh, honey." She tucked her hair behind her ears, smoothing the gray-streaked strands. "There's no way I can do that."

"Why? Because you think she's right? Because you think I'm the one who should relocate?"

"This isn't about who's willing to move and where they should go. This is about two people who need to learn to compromise, to work through their problems together."

"Easy for you to say."

"No. This isn't easy for me at all. I love you and Tamra. I want both of you to be happy."

"Well, we're not. We're making each other miserable."

Mary sighed. "When you were a little boy and you were sad, you used to put your head on my lap. But you're a grown man now, and I don't know how to make you feel better."

"I wish I was a kid. Life was simpler then."

"Was it?" she asked. "Are you sure about that?"

"No." His life had never been simple, especially after he'd lost his parents. He gazed into her eyes, tempted to lay his head on her lap, to go back in time and start over. He wished he could remember her, that his memories weren't so scattered. He even carried the family photo he'd copied in his wallet, but that hadn't changed him. It hadn't renewed his identity. "I don't even know who I am anymore."

She touched his cheek. "You're the man Tamra loves."

"But it hurts, Mom."

"I know." She traced the angles of his face, memorizing his features, skimming his unshaved jaw. "She's hurting, too."

"And I promised her that wouldn't happen."

"If you search deep enough, you'll find a solution. Look at Charlotte and Alexandre. Look how they've managed to be together." She lowered her hand. "Alexandre has vineyards and a home in France. But he's content to stay in America until Charlotte is ready to move. And even then, they'll still have this house. They'll still have ties in Napa Valley."

"It's not the same thing."

"Yes, it is. But you're just too mixed up to see it. Give yourself some time. Think through it. Make peace with yourself. With everything and everyone around you, if that's what it takes."

It was honest advice. Advice from the heart. But Walker didn't know how to heed it. Although there were other disturbances in his life, they didn't compare to what was happening with Tamra.

Without thinking, he dropped his head to Mary's lap. And this time, when she touched his cheek, he closed his eyes. "I don't want Tamra to leave."

"She doesn't want to lose you, either. But she's as mixed up as you are."

"Then we'll never figure it out."

"Yes, you will," his mother said. "If you love each other enough, you will."

Eleven

On the day Tamra was scheduled to leave, she awakened at dawn with a fog-shrouded morning light filling the room.

She rolled over and looked at Walker. He was still asleep. He wore a pair of boxer shorts, and his hair was tousled in restless disarray. One arm was flung over his face, and the covers, which he'd kicked away, were bunched below his hips.

She wanted to move closer, to touch him, to hold him, but she kept her distance. Although they were still sharing the same bed in his Ashton Estate apartment, they hadn't made love since that fateful night in San Francisco.

The night she'd lost him.

But she knew it was her fault. She'd rejected Walker's invitation. She'd refused to live with him, to share his life.

And now she was paying the price.

He shifted in his sleep, moving his arm away from his face, exposing hard angles and handsome features.

Tamra pulled her side of the covers against her body, trying to warm the self-induced chill in her bones. She knew she was making a mistake, yet she didn't know how to repair the damage, how to stay with the man she loved.

He stirred again, and when he opened his eyes, her heart nearly stopped.

"Hi," she said, for lack of a better greeting.

"Hi." He didn't smile, but neither did she.

Instead they simply gazed at each other. For the past few days they'd barely talked, barely communicated beyond forced conversations. Yet neither of them had suggested that they should sleep in separate rooms.

It was insane, she knew, to stay in the same bed, but it was their choice. Their own personal punishment. A need they couldn't deny.

He broke eye contact, glancing at the clock. "It's early."

She knew what he meant. Too early to get ready for the airport. "Do you want some coffee? I can make a pot."

"Sure, I guess." He sat up and smoothed his hair.

She noticed that he hadn't shaved in days. That his jaw was peppered with a coarse texture. But not too coarse. Walker didn't have a heavy beard.

"Are you hungry?" she asked.

"Not really. Are you?"

"No. But I'll probably make some toast. I don't like to drink coffee on an empty stomach."

"Me, neither."

"Then I'll fix some toast for you, too."

As she climbed out of bed, she could feel him watching her. The masculine scrutiny made her self-conscious. She wanted to grab a robe to cover her nightgown, but she didn't have one handy. So she left the room with her pulse pounding in her breast.

When she returned from the kitchen with coffee and buttered toast, Walker was still in bed, still wearing his boxers. She set their breakfast on the nightstand, and he thanked her in a quiet voice.

Tamra reached for her cup, then tasted her drink, trying to think of something to say. "It's a gloomy day," she managed.

His voice turned rough. "It fits my mood." He paused, his gaze searching hers. "It's going to feel strange after you're gone."

"For me, too." She let out the breath she was holding. "Why don't you come back to the rez for the powwow next week? Your sister and Alexandre will be there, and—"

"I can't," he interjected. "I can't take any more time off from Ashton-Lattimer, at least not so soon. I'm behind as it is."

"I understand," she told him, her heart sinking to her stomach.

He glanced at the window, at the fog drifting across the glass. "Maybe I shouldn't go to the airport today." He dropped crumbs onto the sheet, but he didn't bother to dust them off. "Charlotte and Alexandre offered to drive you and Mom, and that might be easier. I don't think I can handle a long goodbye."

Her heart remained in her stomach. "It's okay."

"Are you sure?"

"Yes," she said, even though she wanted him to be there, to walk her as far as the airport security would allow, to pretend that he was traveling with her. "It's fine, Walker. You can stay home."

Three hours later Tamra was packed and ready to leave. Or almost ready, she amended. Lilah had insisted that everyone gather in the dining room for a breakfast-style brunch.

So the Ashton family and their departing guests socialized, with eggs, bacon and strawberry crepes on their plates. Mary, Charlotte and Alexandre spoke to Paige and Trace, while Lilah added champagne to her orange juice.

Tamra didn't eat much. The toast and coffee she'd consumed earlier had been more than enough. Walker didn't appear to have an appetite, either. He simply moved the food around on his plate.

Finally, the meal ended, and Alexandre announced that it was time to leave for the airport.

Soft-spoken farewells were exchanged. Lilah did the best she could, trying to ease the tension. After she gave Mary a peck on the cheek, Spencer's widow offered Tamra a check, a donation for the Oyate Project. Tamra thanked the dazzling redhead, realizing Walker must have told his aunt about the Lakota charity.

Walker said goodbye to Mary first. He embraced her, holding her gently in his arms, promising her that he would keep in touch as often as he could, proving how far he and Mary had come. They were, without a doubt, mother and son.

Tears welled up in Tamra's eyes, but she kept them at bay, refusing to cry in front of everyone.

When Walker turned to her, she waited for him to make the first move, to touch her.

And then time stopped. He brushed his mouth across hers, and suddenly they were the only two people on earth.

She melted against him, her knees going girlishly weak.

"I'm sorry," she whispered, apologizing for not making their relationship work, for not finding a way to be together.

"I'm sorry, too," he said.

She put her head on his shoulder, asking the Creator to give her strength, to let him go without dying inside. But her prayer didn't work.

They separated, and he stepped back, leaving her empty inside.

But that didn't change what was happening. Within seconds it was over. They said goodbye, and Tamra walked out the door and climbed into Alexandre's car, sitting next to Mary in the backseat.

Battling the ache in her chest, she glanced out the

window, wondering if Walker had followed them. But he was nowhere to be seen.

He'd disappeared. Just like the morning fog.

A week later Walker sat in a San Francisco bar, waiting for Trace to arrive. He'd asked his cousin to meet him, but Trace hadn't shown up yet.

He checked his watch. He'd been nursing the same beer for twenty minutes. Not that he cared. He'd chosen a rowdy bar with billiard tables and a blaring jukebox because he needed to be around the activity, to blend in with the noise.

Walker had been working a grueling schedule, putting in even longer hours than usual, but once his day finally ended, he couldn't bear to go home to an empty condo.

He glanced up and spotted Trace coming through the door. His cousin seemed irritated, as if he'd been stuck in traffic.

They made eye contact across the wood-grain room, and Trace approached him, the scowl on his face making him look tough, which was exactly what he was.

An angry Ashton.

"You better have a damn good reason for this meeting," he said, taking a moment to glance around. "And besides that, you couldn't have picked a nicer location? This place is a dive."

"Sit down and shut up," Walker told him, wondering if he'd made a mistake. He and Trace hadn't said a civil word to each other in years. "Let me buy you a beer and we'll get this over with."

"Fine. Whatever." Trace pulled up a chair. In the dim light, his green eyes looked catlike. Wary, sharp, distrustful.

A cocktail waitress, a forty-something brunette, came by and took their order. And soon they both had fresh drinks in front of them. The peanuts on the table remained untouched.

"So what's this all about?" Trace asked.

"It's personal."

"I just drove an hour for an answer like that? Personal how? And what's it got to do with me?"

"I'm trying to make peace with myself, and my mom told me that I should make peace with the people around me, too. So I figured I'd start with you."

"Is this a joke?" His cousin glanced around for a hidden camera. "Or something you did just to piss me off?"

Walker cursed beneath his breath. It did sound rather stupid now that he'd said it out loud. "I'm going through a rough time. I didn't know what else to do."

"I'm not good at giving advice. But if you need a sounding board, go ahead." The other man took a swig of his beer, then sat upright in his chair. "I'm game."

No way, Walker thought. He wasn't about to tell Trace how much he missed Tamra. He wasn't about to admit that he couldn't sleep at night. Or that his chest felt like a limestone cavern, a gaping hole where his heart used to be.

"Well," Trace prodded. "Spill your guts."

"So you can watch me suffer? That wasn't what I had in mind."

His cousin made a stoic expression, something he did far too often. Walker never knew what Trace was thinking. He was good at masking his emotions.

"I don't even know why I dislike you," Walker said. "Other than you were a pest when you were a kid."

That almost made Trace smile. Almost. "I'm four years younger than you. What did you expect?"

"Was it Spencer? Was he the problem? Did he make us enemies?"

"Because you were Dad's protégé?" Trace shelled a peanut. "That didn't help."

"It wasn't a fair fight. Spencer treated me better than he treated you."

"Yes, but considering what he did to you, lying about your mom, I think he evened the score. Dad didn't love anyone but himself."

Love. The word bounced off Walker's hollow chest. He'd wanted Spencer to love him. So much so, he'd buried his memories, pretending that Mary and David—his own parents—had never existed.

"Dad did something deceitful to me, too," Trace said.

"He did?"

His cousin nodded. "I was never close to him to begin with, but the real animosity started when he bought off my fiancée."

Walker thought about the money Spencer had given Mary. Apparently that was the older man's answer to everything. "He paid the woman you loved? Why? To get her out of your life?"

"A hundred grand."

"He gave my mom a lousy thirty."

Trace blew out an exhausted breath, and they both drank their beers. He wondered if his cousin still loved his fiancée. "Did your lady take the money?"

"Every dime."

Walker frowned. He barely remembered that Trace had been engaged. He'd never given a damn about other people's lives. He'd been too busy kissing Spencer's butt. "Do you think I'm like him?"

"Who? My dad? You modeled yourself after him, didn't you? Hell, you're even taking his place at the office. Filling his shoes."

Suddenly the image of living in Spencer's shadow made Walker ill. He wanted to be his own man, his own person, to find the peace his mother had talked about. But instead, he was the CEO at Ashton-Lattimer, paying himself off, the way Spencer had paid off Trace's fiancée. "I'm sorry about what he did to you."

"It was five years ago. I'm over it now."

Liar, Walker thought. Trace was still hurting. Somewhere in the depth of those catlike eyes, his cousin's pain was brewing, waiting to explode. "Do you think your dad is still messing with our minds? Even from the grave?"

Trace didn't respond, but it didn't matter. Walker already knew the answer. At least for himself. He'd chosen Ashton-Lattimer over Tamra.

And now he wanted to right the wrongs, to make their relationship work, to be with her. But it wasn't as simple as quitting his job. There were other compromises to make. And he couldn't make them alone.

He needed Tamra to cooperate.

The following day Walker arrived on the rez. He'd stopped by his mom's house, but no one was home. And that's when he'd remembered the powwow. So here he was, overwhelmed by the festivities. Everywhere he turned, there was something happening.

Beneath an endless sea of canopies, families gathered in lawn chairs, watching regalia-draped dancers spin in colorful circles. In another congested area, craft-booth vendors peddled their wares and food stands created mouthwatering aromas. But that wasn't the last of it. Nestled in tree-clustered corners, storytellers captured the imaginations of wide-eyed children, who sat cross-legged in the grass, listening with rapt attention.

While Walker scanned the grounds, the host Drum sang a traditional song, the music thumping like a heartbeat, drifting through the sun-warmed air.

Feathers, fringe and fry bread, he thought. He had no idea where to look for Tamra. He assumed his mom and his sister were here, too. And Alexandre, of course, making him wonder what the Frenchman thought of the Pine Ridge gathering. No doubt, he and Charlotte were having the time of their lives.

A group of teenagers skirted past Walker, flirting shamelessly with each other. He smiled to himself, then battled a pang of nervousness.

What if Tamra didn't accept his proposition? What

if she didn't think his idea had merit? There would be sacrifices to make, changes to consider, an unconventional future that might leave her wanting more.

He'd rehearsed his upcoming speech last night, going over the details in his mind, but now he wished he had called ahead and warned Tamra that he was coming.

A bit lost, Walker stood in the middle of the powwow grounds, turning in every direction, searching for her.

"If it isn't the yummy *iyeska*," a voice said from behind him.

He spun around and found Michele, Tamra's loyal friend, grinning at him. He smiled, too, grateful to see a familiar face. She sported a jingle dress, the fabric covered with cones made from the metal lids of snuff cans. Her accessories included a silver belt, beaded moccasins and matching leggings. In her hair, she wore a lone feather, held in place with a decorative ornament.

"I didn't know you were a competition dancer," he said, noticing the number attached to her regalia.

"And I didn't know you were going to be here." She tilted her head. "I wonder why Tamra didn't say anything."

His nerves kicked in again. "She doesn't know."

Michele's eyes lit up. "You came here to surprise her? Well, thank goodness. That girl has been miserable."

Relief washed over him. Miserable meant that she missed him. Or so he hoped. "Where is she?"

"Walking around, selling raffle tickets." Michele gestured with her lips. "But I just saw your mom at a fry bread stand. She introduced me to your sister and that hunk of burning love she's gonna marry. Boy, is he a charmer."

"Alexandre knows how to impress the ladies."

"I'll say."

He gazed in the direction of the food stands. "Do you think my mom is still there?"

"Probably. The line was pretty long." She shifted the pouch over her arm. "I'm really glad you came back. I hope you stick around this time."

"I plan to. Sort of," he added, his pulse pounding at his throat. "I'll see you around, okay? I'm going to go talk to my mom."

"Sure. Okay," she said, giving him an obscure look. Apparently his "sort of" comment confused her.

But Walker didn't have time to explain. If he didn't find Tamra soon, his anxiety would probably escalate into a full-blown panic attack.

He found Mary, Charlotte and Alexandre easily, realizing he'd probably walked past them a dozen times. His mom was thrilled to see him. She threw her arms around him, and he nuzzled her neck, grateful that she was part of his life. He still didn't remember her. But he'd loved her. He knew that now, as sure as he knew his own name. He could feel the connection they shared, the bond Spencer had tried to break.

She stepped back to study him. "My son. My boy. I can't believe you're here."

"Iná." He addressed her in Lakota and made her smile.

"Did you come for Tamra?"

He nodded, wishing his stomach would quit flopping back and forth. "But I can't find her."

"Then I'll help you."

Although Mary was familiar with the powwow grounds, it didn't prove to be an easy task. They strolled the festivities for at least fifteen minutes, weaving in and out of the crowd.

Then finally Mary got his attention. "There she is."

He stopped, frozen in his tracks. Tamra was about twenty feet away, near a craft booth, selling raffle tickets to a group of tourists.

His mom squeezed his arm. "I think you can take it from here."

He nodded, although Tamra hadn't spotted him yet. "I love you," he whispered to his mom, wanting her to know how much she meant to him.

"I love you, too," she whispered back, a smile touching her lips, a maternal glow shimmering in her eyes. Then she left him alone, encouraging him to approach Tamra, to try to change the course of their lives.

Tamra finished her transaction, and he moved closer. She caught sight of him and gasped.

For a suspended moment in time, they stared at each other. Then she came toward him. She wore a pair of faded jeans, a sleeveless blouse tied at her waist and the tan cowboys boots he'd become accustomed to seeing. Behind her, hills rose in the distance, creating a sacred backdrop.

Mother Earth and the lady he loved.

He wanted to latch on to her and never let go, but he steadied his hands instead, cramming them into his pockets.

"You said you weren't coming to the powwow." Her voice all but quavered. "But here you are."

Yes, here he was, so nervous he could barely speak. He cleared his throat. "Can you take a break?"

"Yes, of course." She fidgeted with the roll of tickets in her hand.

He guided her to a vacant spot on the grass, and they sat on the ground, with the summer heat glaring between them. Her hair fell to her shoulders in a glossy black sheen, and her exotic-shaped eyes tilted at the corners. Around her neck, she wore a beaded medicine wheel, a symbol that represented the four directions and the four cardinal Lakota values: integrity, bravery, fortitude and generosity.

Walker thought it suited her beautifully.

"I'm leaving Ashton-Lattimer," he said. "I don't want to fill Spencer's shoes. I don't want to live the rest of my life in his shadow."

Her gaze locked on his. "What are you going to do?"

"Start my own financial consulting firm."

"In San Francisco?"

"Yes, but I intend to find a partner. Someone who can handle the day-to-day operation, who can run the company when I'm not around." He took a chance, moving closer to her. "That way I can commute between here and there. Live in both places."

Her eyelashes fluttered, and he realized she was

blinking back tears. "Both places? Does that mean we can be together?"

"Yes, but it won't be easy. Not at first," he told her, refusing to sugarcoat the situation, to be anything less than honest. "I'll be putting in long hours, getting the new company started. But eventually I'll get my schedule squared away."

"So you can spend more time here? With me?" she asked, her gaze hopeful, her voice soft.

He nodded, thinking how delicate she seemed. But he'd caught her off guard, probably sending her tattered emotions into a tailspin. "I'm not expecting you to quit your job for me. I know how much the Oyate Project means to you, how important it is to the rez. But I was hoping that you'd come to California once in a while. On your days off or whenever you can manage it."

"I'm willing to do whatever it takes," she said, reaching for him. "I can't bear to lose you again."

He took her in his arms, and when she trembled against him, he stroked her hair. He could feel how much she loved him, how lonely she'd been without him by her side. But even so, he wanted her to be sure.

"Our lives won't be as conventional as most couples, Tamra. I'll be gone a lot. Probably a few weeks a month."

She lifted her head. "That doesn't matter to me. Not if we make a commitment to each other, promises we both intend to keep." She sat back, pressed a hand to her heart. "This is the answer to our prayers, Walker. It's the perfect solution. We need to blend our worlds to make this work."

"Does spending more time in San Francisco scare you?" he asked. "The way adapting to reservation life scares me?"

She released a choppy breath. "Yes, but you can teach me to appreciate the city, to see it through your eyes. And I can help you get settled on the rez, to make it seem like home."

A feeling of contentment settled over him. Substance, he thought. Compromise, the beauty of commitment, of making every moment count. "We're going to need a bigger house. My mom's place is too small."

She smiled. "Does that mean we're going to live with Mary?"

He smiled, too. "It seems like the most logical solution. That way, neither of you will be alone when I'm in California."

"A new house is fine, but nothing too fancy. Don't go overboard."

"When I want fancy, I'll go to the estate and hobnob with the Ashtons. Besides, I'm keeping my condo. I'll have plenty of luxury when I need it." He paused, felt his heart bump his chest. "We can do this. We can make it happen."

She looked into his eyes. "I love you, Walker."

"I love you, too." He took her in his arms again, knowing she was accepting him for who he was.

A Pine Ridge Lakota. A San Francisco *iyeska*.

He was both of those things. Both people. But most of all, he was Tamra's partner, the man who couldn't live without her.

* * *

In the wee hours of the morning, Tamra and Walker were still awake. They were in her room, cuddling and talking, too wired to sleep.

Tamra couldn't stop looking at him, touching him, feeling his skin beneath her fingers. For her this was a dream. A real-life fairy tale, something she never expected.

"What kind of wedding do you want?" he asked.

"Wedding?" Her pulse jumped. "You never said anything about us getting married."

He raised his eyebrows. "Did you think I was asking you to live in sin?"

She laughed and pinched his side, making him laugh, too. "That's a hell of a proposal."

He toyed with the ends of her hair. "Glad you think so."

She couldn't help but smile. They were side by side, half-dressed and full of emotion. "Are we going to have a long engagement or is this supposed to happen fast?"

"A long engagement," he decided. "We should do it right. Maybe even have two ceremonies. One here and one on the estate."

"That works for me. If we're going to blend our worlds, we should get married in both places."

"My thoughts exactly." His expression changed, turning a bit troubled.

Concerned, she studied the angles of his face, the hard lines and deep, dark shadows. "What's wrong?"

"I have no idea what's going to happen with the stocks I inherited. They'll probably be held up in probate for a long time, especially if Eli or somebody from that side of the family contests the will."

"Do the stocks matter all that much?"

"Not really. Not anymore. I'd just sell them, anyway." He propped himself up, leaning on one elbow. "I have other investments I can liquidate."

"To get your business started?"

"To help the rez. I'd like to establish a housing fund, maybe work with a local contractor who's willing to get involved."

Her heart all but melted. "To help solve the housing shortage?"

He nodded. "Even if it's just one or two houses a year. Whatever I can manage. Whatever I can do to make a difference."

"No wonder I love you so much." She took a deep breath, searched his gaze, broaching a subject they'd both been avoiding. "How are other things going? Are you sorting out your feelings for Spencer?"

Walker frowned. "I'm trying to come to terms with what he did, with how many people he hurt. But that doesn't mean I condone his murder. I want to know who killed him." He adjusted the blanket, smoothing a ripple in the fabric. "As for my childhood memories, I'm convinced they'll come back."

"I think so, too." Once again she studied him. A pale-blue lamp bathed him in a translucent glow, creating the illusion of twilight, of moonbeams dancing across his skin. "What about children?" she asked suddenly, realizing it was a topic they hadn't discussed. "Do you want kids?"

He reached for her hand. "Anytime you're ready."

She clasped her fingers through his, awed by his beauty, his masculine strength, the passion, the tenderness, the complexity of his personality. "I'd prefer to be married first."

"Then we'll wait." His voice turned quiet. "Would it be all right to alter Jade's headstone? To give her my last name, too?"

Tamra's eyes misted. "Are you asking to be her father?"

"If you don't mind."

She thought about her baby, about the teddy bear, the lamb, the delicate pink roses. "I'd be honored."

He leaned in to kiss her, and she welcomed his embrace, the strength of his touch. She liked being protected by him.

When he slipped his tongue into her mouth, she sighed. He tasted like mint, like the toothpaste he'd used. Fresh and clean and cool.

Their hands were still entwined, connected like a jigsaw puzzle. Pieces that fit. Pieces that belonged together.

Their eyes met, and she knew he was thinking about their future. She was thinking about it, too.

"Forever," she whispered.

"Forever," he repeated, removing what was left of her clothes, running his hands over her body, his fingers seeking, taking possession, claiming every inch of her flesh.

She arched and sighed, and he made love with her, as slowly as they both could endure. Warm and willing, he moved inside her, the rhythm as deep and erotic as a river, as a current flowing through her womb.

She closed her eyes, inhaling his scent, memorizing his pheromones in her mind. As he touched her, she took in every sensation, every wondrous caress.

Spellbound, she floated, her bones and her muscles melting beneath him. Such weightless pleasure, she thought. Reality, fantasy. Everything a woman could want.

She opened her eyes, looked at him, saw him looking back at her.

His body trembled for hers. She could feel his need, his hunger, the power of being loved, of the vow they'd made.

He increased the tempo, going deeper, thrusting on a dream, on sex and sin and everything in between. She clung to his shoulders, wrapping her legs around his waist.

When it happened, when he came, she let him carve a groove right into her soul. She climaxed, too, absorbing the milky warmth that was part of him.

Minutes later they lay in each other's arms, basking in the afterglow. Her hair was still tangled around his fingers, and her hand rested dangerously close to his thigh.

She pressed her lips to his neck and smiled. He was still hard, still partially aroused, even after what they'd done. "I'm going to like being engaged to you."

He returned her smile. "Just think of how desperate we're going to be for each other when I'm not around."

"We'll make up for it every time you come back." Here, she thought. To the rez. The place that held her heart. But that wasn't all of it. She'd agreed to be part of his existence, too. Part of the places that held his heart. "I can't believe I'm going to be a full-fledged Ashton. Flying to San Francisco whenever I can. Attending parties on the estate."

He shook his head. "We've created quite a situation for ourselves, haven't we?"

Silent, she nodded. She knew it wasn't a simple life they'd chosen. But it was their decision, their way of being together. And she wouldn't trade it for anything. Walker Ashton belonged to her and she belonged to him.

Anxious to kiss him again, she rolled over, straddling his lap. He grinned and pulled her closer.

But before she could cover his mouth with hers, he tickled her, sending her into a girlish fit, making her laugh, making her feel happy and free.

Thrilled to be with him.

The man she would always love.

From now until the end of time.

* * * * *

Watch for the next installment of
DYNASTIES: THE ASHTONS, *Kristi Gold's*
MISTAKEN FOR A MISTRESS, available
in August from Silhouette Desire.

Silhouette Desire®

Available this August from
Silhouette Desire and *USA TODAY*
bestselling author

Jennifer Greene

HOT TO THE TOUCH
(Silhouette Desire #1670)

Locked in the darkness of his tortured soul and
body, Fox Lockwood has tried to retreat from
the world. Hired to help, massage therapist
Phoebe Schneider relies on her sense of touch
to bring Fox back. But will they be able to keep
their relationship strictly professional once their
connection turns unbelievably hot?

Available wherever Silhouette Books are sold.

If you enjoyed what you just read,
then we've got an offer you can't resist!

Take 2 bestselling
love stories FREE!

Plus get a FREE surprise gift!

Clip this page and mail it to Silhouette Reader Service™

IN U.S.A.
3010 Walden Ave.
P.O. Box 1867
Buffalo, N.Y. 14240-1867

IN CANADA
P.O. Box 609
Fort Erie, Ontario
L2A 5X3

YES! Please send me 2 free Silhouette Desire® novels and my free surprise gift. After receiving them, if I don't wish to receive anymore, I can return the shipping statement marked cancel. If I don't cancel, I will receive 6 brand-new novels every month, before they're available in stores! In the U.S.A., bill me at the bargain price of **$3.80** plus 25¢ shipping and handling per book and applicable sales tax, if any*. In Canada, bill me at the bargain price of $4.47 plus 25¢ shipping and handling per book and applicable taxes**. That's the complete price and a savings of at least 10% off the cover prices—what a great deal! I understand that accepting the 2 free books and gift places me under no obligation ever to buy any books. I can always return a shipment and cancel at any time. Even if I never buy another book from Silhouette, the 2 free books and gift are mine to keep forever.

225 SDN DZ9F
326 SDN DZ9G

Name	(PLEASE PRINT)
Address	Apt.#
City	State/Prov.	Zip/Postal Code

Not valid to current Silhouette Desire® subscribers.

Want to try two free books from another series?
Call 1-800-873-8635 or visit www.morefreebooks.com.

* Terms and prices subject to change without notice. Sales tax applicable in N.Y.
** Canadian residents will be charged applicable provincial taxes and GST.
All orders subject to approval. Offer limited to one per household.
® are registered trademarks owned and used by the trademark owner and or its licensee.

DES04R   ©2004 Harlequin Enterprises Limited

Silhouette® Desire®

brings you a fabulous new read
from popular author

Katherine Garbera

She's an up-and-coming DJ who gives advice
to the lovelorn…but has no time for romance.

He's a hotshot bachelor who's suddenly
intrigued by a voice on the radio.

The late-night airwaves are about to get
a little bit hotter.…

ROCK ME ALL NIGHT
August 2005

Available at your favorite retail outlet.

THE SECRET DIARY

A new drama unfolds for six of the state's wealthiest bachelors.

This newest installment continues with

LESS-THAN-INNOCENT INVITATION

by Shirley Rogers

(Silhouette Desire #1671)

Melissa Mason will do almost anything to avoid talking to her former fiancé, Logan Voss. Too bad his ranch is the only place she can stay while in Royal. What's worse, he seems determined to renew their acquaintance… in every way.

Available August 2005 at your favorite retail outlet.

COMING NEXT MONTH

#1669 MISTAKEN FOR A MISTRESS—Kristi Gold
Dynasties: The Ashtons
To solve his grandfather's murder, Ford Ashton concealed his true identity to seduce his grandfather's suspected mistress. But he soon discovered that Kerry Rourke was not all *she* appeared to be. Her offer to help him find the truth turned his mistrust to attraction. Yet even if they solved the case, could love survive with so much deception between them?

#1670 HOT TO THE TOUCH—Jennifer Greene
Fox Lockwood was suffering from a traumatic war experience no doctor could cure. Enter Phoebe Schneider—a masseuse specializing in soothing distraught infants. But Fox was fully grown, and though Phoebe desired to relieve his tension, dare she risk allowing their professional relationship to take a more personal turn?

#1671 LESS-THAN-INNOCENT INVITATION—Shirley Rogers
Texas Cattleman's Club: The Secret Diary
When Melissa Mason heard rancher Logan Voss proposed to her simply to secure his family inheritance, she ended their engagement and broke his heart. Ten years later, now an accomplished news reporter, Melissa had accepted an assignment that brought her back to Logan, forcing her to confront the real reason she left all they had behind.

#1672 ROCK ME ALL NIGHT—Katherine Garbera
King of Hearts
Dumped by her fiancé on New Year's Eve, late-night DJ Lauren Belchoir had plenty to vent to her listeners about romance. But when hip record producer Jack Montrose appeared, passion surged between them like high-voltage airwaves. Would putting their hearts on the air determine if their fairy-tale romance was real, or just after-hours gossip?

#1673 SEDUCTION BY THE BOOK—Linda Conrad
The Gypsy Inheritance
Widower Nicholas Scoville had isolated himself on his Caribbean island—until beautiful Annie Riley arrived and refused to be ignored. One long night, one vivid storm and some mindless passion later…could what they found in each other's arms overcome Nick's painful past?

#1674 HER ROYAL BED—Laura Wright
She had been a princess only a month before yearning for her old life. So when Jane Hefner Al-Nayhal traveled to Texas to see her brother and a detour landed her in the arms of cowboy Bobby Callahan, she began thinking of taking a permanent vacation. But Bobby had planned to destroy her family. Was Jane's love strong enough to prevent disaster?

SDCNM0705